Letter of Intent

LETTER OF INTENT

URSULA CURTISS

A Red Badge Novel of Suspense

DODD, MEAD & COMPANY · NEW YORK

ISBN 0-396-06356-X
Library of Congress Catalog Card Number: 70-145394
Printed in the United States of America
by Vail-Ballou Press, Inc., Binghamton, N. Y.

The harmless-looking white envelope with her name and room number printed on it in pencil was delivered by a bellboy at six o'clock on that cold January evening. He was a new and very conscientious bellboy, and volunteered that the envelope had just been discovered at the desk; he didn't think it could have been there long.

The woman in 218 opened it with only mechanical interest, because the two little flourishes with which her name had been underlined did not, so far, carry either mockery or menace. Face grown stupid with shock as the years fell away, she read the brief printed message: "I've been waiting for this. If you don't call off the wedding, I will."

There was no signature; her world was to be blown to pieces by a gloved hand. No, she thought, almost crystal with rage. *No.*

It was a convulsive reaction that made her tear the envelope and the single sheet of paper into small pieces and burn them in the generous bedside ashtray before she flushed them away. Then, automatically, she wiped the smoky glass until it shone again. The very activity, the fact of having sent this dreadful thing into permanent oblivion, helped to slow her racing heart and collect her wits.

A warning implied a grace period. Surely, if she thought hard enough, she could identify *who* . . . ?

And do something about it. Tonight.

One

Mrs. James Stevenson was a woman of poise and experience, and did not at all dread the breaking-in of a new young maid; if anything, she felt it a challenge. "You'll be Celia," she said briskly, welcoming the girl on a dark and dripping winter morning. "Goodness, you're wet! If you had called half an hour ago Mr. Stevenson could have met you at the station."

There was no response in the rather square face under the heavily braided pale-blonde hair, although the word "wet" seemed to have registered; the girl began to unbutton her brown coat with uncertain fingers.

"That's it," said Mrs. Stevenson encouragingly, making a lightning assessment of the figure that emerged. Tall, big-boned, obviously healthy; probably younger than the eighteen she was purported to be. Her apparent bewilderment must be a language difficulty, compounded by Mrs. Stevenson's English accent, because there was nothing slow about the dark eyes—indeed, they were making an almost disconcerting assessment in return.

The impression of—was intelligence the proper word?—was quickly borne out. Celia, whose consonant-laden last name Mrs. Stevenson never mastered, was an apt and even anxious pupil. Within a week she had breakfast on the table exactly as the Stevensons liked it, in three weeks she could serve dinner without an air of painful concentration. And, an attribute her employer found rarer than rubies, she did not break things. Her hands were so deft and sure that for the first time in years Mrs. Stevenson relinquished the care of the Coalport china and the good wine glasses.

The weeks became months, and Celia still did not demand extra time off or complain because there was no television set in her room. Mrs. Stevenson might almost have thought her too good to be true if she were not matter-of-factly aware that the working conditions were pleasant; in fact, she never had to seek the offices of employment agencies, as maids who departed because of marital or other family problems always had a relative to volunteer. As an employer, she herself was firm but good-tempered, and took a genuine interest in the well-being of anyone who worked for her. For most of the time, although their married daughter came for an occasional visit with her children, and their son was periodically home from college, the household consisted of Mr. and Mrs. Stevenson and a very well-behaved French poodle.

For her part, Celia was more than content. The fact of a bedroom not shared with two younger sisters was a luxury in itself, and for a long time she was amazed that there were never any shouted quarrels, let alone physical abuse, under the Stevenson roof; for the first few days she supposed that her employers were simply not speaking to each other. Far from resenting Mrs. Stevenson's brisk suggestions as to her appearance, she seized upon them. She did not even mind parting with a good deal of her heavy hair, and she stopped eating potatoes and bread and attacked raw carrots and apples.

Most of all, hardly aware that she did so, she observed. She took meticulous note of Mrs. Stevenson's smallest behavior—at the telephone, with guests, giving instructions to the weekly cleaning-woman—and when her employers entertained, usually at cocktails, she discovered how the little napkins and the toothpicks from tiny hot sausages were dealt with. It took her months to sort out the baffling occasions upon which even women rose to their feet, but she gathered quickly that to linger on a doorstep, chatting instead of taking a crisp departure, was one of the blacker social sins.

When young Hugh Stevenson came home from college for the summer, Celia's education grew much wider. Then the house was full of people hardly older than she, all of whom seemed to possess sports cars. The boys she dismissed, even though she caught an occasional and interested raised eyebrow between them; it was on the girls that she trained her attention. Like a naturalist confronted with a new species, she studied the way they walked and sat and maneuvered themselves into coats held for them; their make-up, or largely lack of it that year; their clothes.

It was the clothes that sent up the first faint smoke-signal.

As the product of a large and poor family, Celia had learned, perforce, how to make primitive alterations on handed-down garments. When she had been with the Stevensons for a year and a half, she asked Mrs. Stevenson to teach her to sew. There was a machine, seldom used, in the daughter's bedroom, and Mrs. Stevenson was pleased at this evidence of enterprise. Celia took well to instruction—her neat-handedness had never been more to the fore—and made first a pillow slip, then a cotton shift from a pattern, then, recklessly, a dress from a length of beautiful avocado-gold brocade. It was almost as simple in line as the shift, and the seams were dubious, but in it Celia was someone else. She was One of Those Girls.

She never went home on her day off now, but sent a terse few dollars a week instead. Home was an ugly husk she had shed, a place full of noise and hungrily outstretched hands. In the town she was not a maid but a girl lunching in a restaurant while she practiced Mrs. Stevenson's manners, a languid afternoon shopper who rarely bought anything but basked in the attention of salespeople. Occasionally, because it seemed an improving thing to do, she went and sat in a small, green, tree-shadowed park, looking as though she were enjoying nature, before she returned to the Stevensons', fixed herself a small salad in the kitchen, and went upstairs to her room.

On a day in late August, newly slim in her avocado dress, she turned out of the park and was seized about the waist from behind. A male voice deep with laughter said, "Aha! Going to stand me up, were you?" and a kiss landed on the side of her throat before she whirled and stared at the aghast and reddening face of Hugh Stevenson.

"*Celia.* I'm so sorry, I thought you were . . . It must be the dress. I was meeting someone here, and I could have sworn . . . Did I scare you to death?"

They had an audience: a gleeful child, a zestfully attentive old man, a sympathetically smiling couple with a

6

cocker spaniel on a leash. Celia said primly that it was quite all right and walked away, her throat still blazing from that unexpected contact.

But it was not all right. The smiling couple obviously knew the Stevensons. Celia was dismayed but not altogether surprised when, a calculated week later, Mrs. Stevenson said with brisk pleasantness, "I'll hate to lose you, Celia, but a friend of mine is ill and in need of someone competent to help out . . ."

Two

Celia did not like the Strykers at all. The wife was a vain and silly hypochondriac who felt that back rubs were the routine duty of a maid; the husband, a florid fifty, was given to standing too close and remaining lodged in doorways so that it was necessary to press past him.

Although their menage was on the surface more opulent than the Stevensons'—there was an unfriendly cook—it was full of little meannesses. There was margarine instead of butter for the servants, and a narrow eye was kept on Mr. Stryker's imported marmalade. As Mrs. Stryker lived in fear that her handsome rugs would fade, heavy draperies were drawn at the offending hours of the morning and afternoon, plunging the house into a funereal gloom.

Nor was all marital harmony. The Strykers, perhaps because of his wandering eye and her imaginary illnesses, kept up a constant low-level bickering which was far more wearing than an occasional explosive scene. Celia discovered that she was the fourth new maid in less than a year.

8

Almost any situation could be turned to advantage, and she made up her mind at once to become indispensable to this querulous pair. She frequently told Mrs. Stryker that she looked tired, at which the invalid would snatch up a mirror and regard herself with morose satisfaction; and on one occasion in the pantry, when Mr. Stryker's hand ventured too close, she fixed him with a long stare of such grimness that the incident was not repeated. At the end of six months, when she had them both lulled into a sense of security, she boldly demanded, and got, a raise.

She had been at the Strykers' a year when something happened which gave a subtle shape to the future: one of the women guests, a Mrs. Caswell, slipped out to the kitchen after dinner and to the accompaniment of nervous backward glances, offered to better whatever the salary was here. Celia said decorously that she was satisfied with her present situation—which she was, with her employers more or less in the palm of her hand—but something she did not recognize as a feeling of power filled her. Before she went to bed, she took a long appraising look at herself.

The rather heavy girl with faltering English who had arrived at Mrs. Stevenson's kitchen door in a soggy and shapeless coat was gone. Only her shoulders remained broad: hard work, plus an avoidance of starches, had trimmed her waist and hips and legs. In her now-fluent speech, the brand-new words she had learned from Mrs. Stevenson retained their original crisp English accent; she knew that this was piquant, because she had heard it remarked upon, and preserved it with care.

She would never be pretty—her bones were too big for that—but her pale hair had grown back quite a bit from its scissoring, and Mrs. Stryker had not the temerity to demand that she have it cut. If she were to wear it in a chignon, or a French twist . . . She turned her face this way and that before the mirror, gazing slantingly at herself out of the dark eyes that were set a little too flush, giving them a peculiarly liquid look.

She remembered Hugh Stevenson's mistake, and for the first time it became translated into something of significance.

Celia did not regret having refused Mrs. Caswell, but she was not quite the same after that. She had never before been much interested in the actual preparation of food; now she watched with care, and presently mastered, the creation of the baked clams and delicate cheese puffs for which the Strykers' cook was fabled. She listened with sharpened awareness to the kitchen consultations before parties: Mrs. Stryker had the mysterious knack of providing an amplitude with no tired, and tiresome, slices and spoonfuls to be resurrected and disguised with considerable time and labor the next day. It was possibly her only virtue.

Celia no longer squandered her afternoons off by pretending to shop, but spent time in the library poring over books on etiquette, gourmet cooking, wines. She had learned at the Stevensons' that there were occasions for red wine and white, but as this was not her decision she had never bothered to differentiate. Now she did, and committed the shapes of the various glasses to memory.

Perhaps her heightened consciousness of herself as a person rather than a maid played a part in what happened soon after she had received a second raise almost without effort; the Strykers, in their bemusement at having a servant who appeared to be permanent, were subservient themselves. At any rate, on a weekend when there were house guests and Celia was straightening one of the bedrooms, its occupant, a black-haired young woman, entered without warning, strolled to a window, and lit a cigarette in an unhurried way.

"I'll come back, ma'am," said Celia, preparing to withdraw, but the girl said easily, "Oh, no, that's all right, I just want to get a scarf."

She fished a glowing square of silk from a suitcase, but she didn't go. She said in a conversational tone, "Have you been here long, Celia?"

For a moment Celia thought she meant here in this room, but then she realized that the scarf was an excuse and the clear, odd-colored gaze openly appraising. "About a year and a half, ma'am."

"That's a record," said the girl, smiling. "Don't worry, I'm a relative of Mrs. Stryker's—by marriage anyway. What I'm getting at is that you seem so very . . . competent that I wonder if you've ever considered a somewhat different kind of job?"

Celia kept her lashes down over a flare of excitement. "That would depend on the circumstances," she said carefully. "I know this house very well, ma'am, and I think Mrs. Stryker is satisfied with my work."

"She is, very, but it seems to me that you're wasting your abilities here. What I had in mind," said the girl bluntly, "is a very old uncle of mine who lives alone and needs someone to manage his house in other ways than meals and so on." She gestured with the hand that held the cigarette. "Someone to keep pests away—the doctor doesn't want him tired—and provide dinner now and then for a few old friends, and remind him to take his medicine. Things like that. There'd be only light cleaning involved, a woman comes in twice a week. I ought to warn you that he's rather difficult—well, he's eighty-odd—but the pay is quite good and a lot of your time would be your own."

There was a catch somewhere, thought Celia shrewdly. Plums like this did not fall into the hands of maids with only three years' experience. The girl, misinterpreting her silence, said hastily, "He's not an invalid, if that's what you're worried about, and in any case his doctor lives quite close by."

"Here in Connecticut?"

"No, in New Jersey. Oh, I see, your family are here," said the girl a little doubtfully, and Celia nodded. She had not seen her family for two years, but the mere fact of their existence might make a bargaining point if matters should ever come to that. "Well . . . think it over, anyway, and let me know. An interview couldn't do any harm," said the girl in a startlingly exact echo of Celia's own thoughts.

A week later, on her day off, Celia presented herself at the tall narrow front of 4 Stedman Circle in Cherryville, New Jersey.

She had dressed with care for what she knew might be a turning point in her life. She wore a simple white blouse with an old but still-good gray suit which Mrs. Stevenson had given her; it made her look older, and the wide sweep of her shoulders saved it from complete dowdiness. Black calf pumps; black handbag that looked like calf but wasn't. On the train, her gloved hands lay quietly in her lap although her heart was beating as it had the first time she had served eight people at dinner.

She had decided, with the New Jersey flats streaming past the window, that the old man was—what did they call it? Senile?—or semibedridden, in spite of what the girl had said, or downright crazy. It was Celia's view that elderly people with money went crazy more readily than people without—or perhaps could afford to stay out of padded cells longer. There was certainly something very odd about the whole thing, and it was entirely possible that Hester Cannon, the black-haired niece, would not even be there as arranged to make introductions.

But in the meantime Celia was traveling farther than she ever had in her life, and she was aware that her fellow passengers would have been surprised to learn that she was a maid inspecting a new job on her day off. The knowledge gave her a feeling of standing on the edge of some enormous discovery; it was like a vast extension of Hugh Stevenson's blundering kiss.

. . . And here was 4 Stedman Circle, resembling a house from which the other half had been lopped away. Railed steps going up, primly potted shrubs on either side of the door—and then, in response to her finger on the bell, Mrs. Cannon.

"Celia. I'm glad you could come." Voice a little crisper, a little less cordial than in the bedroom at the Strykers': Celia had been expecting this, and the swift up-and-down inspection, and was not taken aback. "Come in, won't you, and meet my uncle, Mr. Tomlinson."

It was a very old-fashioned house, conveying an instant impression of camphor-scented velvet; there was even a bay window with ferns and rubber plants. The man who sat in a wing chair with its back to the light, and who rose courteously to greet Celia, was equally old-fashioned:

pink and silver-haired and fragile-looking, complete with vest and starched collar.

Mrs. Cannon said in the elaborately clear pitch which points out deafness, "Uncle Robert, this is Miss——" and came to a surprised stop; she had never inquired Celia's last name. With a flash of insight, Celia telescoped the difficult syllables. "Brett," she said.

The interview that followed was actually her first, as she had been recommended to Mrs. Stevenson by a second cousin and hired sight unseen, but it seemed to Celia that it was hardly an interview at all: Mrs. Cannon was briskly making up her uncle's mind for him. He certainly didn't appear insane, but was he slightly simple? Apart from a plaintive remark that she looked very young he could hardly have been said to participate in the proceedings at all; from his air of merely polite interest as his niece outlined Celia's duties to her, he might have been listening to domestic arrangements being made for some absent stranger.

His meals, said Mrs. Cannon, were simple and bland on his doctor's orders; there was a diet list tacked up in the kitchen. Celia would do the marketing as well as the cooking, and she would see to it that visitors were not allowed to tire Mr. Tomlinson. Laundry was sent out. A cleaning woman came twice a week, but Celia was to consult Mrs. Cannon about any major services: "Mr. Tomlinson finds it hard to say no." It seemed to Celia that Mr. Tomlinson found it hard to say anything, but perhaps the situation altered when his niece was not around.

All this information was produced at considerable volume, as the old man evidently refused to wear a much-needed hearing aid. Was this a factor in her astonishing

14

selection by Mrs. Cannon; had other, better-qualified housekeepers—because that was what the job amounted to—balked at having to communicate in something just short of a shout? Celia's own enunciation, thanks to her original difficulties with grammatical English, was unusually clear.

She had made up her mind to take the position even before her tour of the house with Mrs. Cannon and the discussion of salary and days off; in fact, barring some insuperable difficulty, that decision had already been taken on the train. She wangled one weekend a month for the supposed purpose of visiting the family to whom she was so deeply attached, and said firmly that she would have to give Mrs. Stryker a month's notice—not out of consideration for the woman, whom she despised, but for the effect of reliability which this would create.

The effect was quite otherwise. Mr. Tomlinson's old pink face lit up almost to radiance, and Mrs. Cannon's yellowy eyes grew sharply annoyed. "That won't be necessary," she said with crispness. "The circumstances are unusual, and I'll explain to Mrs. Stryker. You needn't worry about that at all. Can my uncle expect you by nine o'clock on— let me see, this is Thursday—on Monday morning?"

A train schedule was produced. There would be a taxi waiting, as Celia would have her bags. At this point Mrs. Cannon rose brusquely to her feet with a glance at her watch; there was a suggestion that, having won some obscure battle, she was no longer interested in being civil. The old man extended his hand unexpectedly to Celia— it was chilly and dry and the gesture had the air of a secret pact between them—and she descended the railed steps to the street feeling light and unencumbered.

Just as when, a month after going to work at the Stevensons', she had discarded the lumpy brown coat forever, she had cast off another troublesome layer of herself. Brett, she told herself repeatedly on the way home (and she would find out the necessary steps to make this legal). I am Celia Brett.

Three

Celia settled into 4 Stedman Circle with the caution of a cat who suspects an unseen dog somewhere on the premises.

The cleaning woman would undoubtedly be a mine of information about the situation here, but Celia expected, and got, a certain amount of hostility from that quarter in the beginning. Mrs. Meggs, a surprisingly small fortyish woman with hair dyed varnish brown, simply wished her a cold good-morning on the first day and attacked her own work like a giantess on the rampage.

When she came again later in the week and found that Celia had made no attempt to interfere in her domain, she grudgingly accepted a midmorning cup of coffee and asked, "The niece hire you?" When Celia said yes, Mrs. Meggs gave a significant nod and said nothing more. Celia did not press her.

It was not until the following week, when Celia remarked sympathetically that the vacuum was an unwieldly one, that the cleaning woman's restraint began to slip. "It's as old as the hills *and* gives me a nasty shock every now and again," she said with a snort. "I told Mrs. Cannon we needed a new one, but you wouldn't believe the way that woman can pinch a penny."

"You can't go to Mr. Tomlinson about things like that?"

Mrs. Meggs shook her unlikely brown head with emphasis. "He's not to be bothered, she says. Bothered how? What it is, is the poor old soul can't live forever and she's the only relative. She and that husband of hers will get everything and sell this house. They should worry about the work of keeping it up in the meantime." She paused reflectively, and a small, amazingly sardonic laugh escaped her. "Not that they haven't had their worries lately, and not over new vacuum cleaners either."

Celia was too clever to diminish her own position by prying information from a lesser employee. She commenced a shopping list with every appearance of having lost interest, and Mrs. Meggs could not stand it. Her enjoyable secret popped from her like an overripe fruit from its skin.

Mr. Tomlinson had tended to want to marry his last two housekeepers, women in their healthy and companionable fifties. ("And why not, if he wants to?" demanded Mrs. Meggs argumentatively. "He's a lonely old thing and it's his own business. But she won't have it. She shuffles them off like stray cats.")

And Mrs. Cannon had rightly reasoned that, from the vantage point of eighty-two, anyone of Celia's age was hardly more than a child. That was why Mr. Tomlinson had remarked fretfully that she looked very young. Celia was entertained rather than resentful, and would not quarrel with whatever the motive for bringing her to Stedman Circle. It was refreshing not to have a female employer in residence, and she was somehow convinced that when she was firmly entrenched it would be pleasanter still.

She had not seen Mrs. Cannon since the day of the interview, but performed her tasks as though the black-haired young woman were watching every move. She would have done so in any case: in this—as in other matters—Celia was ruthless, and had nothing but contempt for time-killing servants. It would never have occurred to her, although far more shocking things presently would, to settle down in the kitchen with a magazine when she was theoretically dusting the downstairs rooms.

She had wondered how such a fragile old man would fill his days, and was amazed at how busy he made himself. After he came down to breakfast at nine, an apparently unvarying meal of cooked cereal, three-minute egg, toast and tea, he observed birds in the back garden and took notes; often, in consequence, he wrote letters to bird watchers, all over the country. He read and dealt with his mail before lunch, which was often creamed fish or milk toast, and after a nap he went out on his iron-railed balcony, a Panama tilted over his eyes, and picked up a gold-embossed leather volume.

Sometimes in the afternoon there were the visitors Mrs. Cannon seemed to consider such a health hazard, usually men in their sixties or older but occasionally a young couple. Promptly at six o'clock Celia brought Mr. Tomlinson a ceremonial bourbon and water and the evening paper; promptly at seven she served him thin-sliced chicken or lamb, a puréed vegetable, a bland dessert.

The dining room was small but pretty, with its faded

19

pink-and-white paper and rose velvet curtains, and it seemed to Celia a waste when one old man occupied it. She was actively pleased on the mornings when he told her with an apologetic air that there would be guests for dinner; it was possible then to introduce the herbs and mushrooms and sauces she was impatient to practice with, and to demonstrate her competence to more than one pair of eyes.

At first her evenings off presented something of a problem. She was neither a reader nor a letter writer, and the early retirement hour at Stedman Circle allowed her ample time for hair washing and personal laundry. She could go to a movie, or linger over a little shopping, or even, as on one occasion, enter the cocktail lounge of the Gaylord Hotel and stretch a single drink over an hour. This was not a success: although she had long ago gotten over any nervousness with waiters, she knew herself to be—a young woman out alone in the evening—an object of mild speculation.

On an evening in late November, the free and assured-looking walk which was an accident of muscles and bone structure carried Celia past her usual perimeter. The main doors of a lighted office building opened and people came streaming and chattering out into the cold—mainly young people, Celia realized with an unconscious surprise that came from spending her days largely in the company of Mr. Tomlinson and Mrs. Meggs. She crossed a tiny, windy park and entered the lobby of the building, although overheard scraps of conversation along the way had already told her what she wanted to know. On the second floor, the Fennimore Business School was conducting night classes in shorthand and typing.

20

Celia went thoughtfully back to Stedman Circle.

There were all those letters to fellow bird-watchers, written in Mr. Tomlinson's jagged, meticulous script. On the afternoons when he did not have visitors, he dictated mild opinions about foreign policy, interspersed with reminiscences of World War I, into a tape recorder, and played them back with obvious glee. If he cocked his head and cupped his good ear with such pride, mightn't he be even happier to see his own words in print? On the other hand, there was the vigilant Mrs. Cannon, who would certainly be up in arms at her uncle's paying for his housekeeper's typing lessons—because Celia had no intention of paying for them herself.

Neither did she want to lose this position. She mulled the matter over for a week, and it was a second wintry walk to the little park and the spilling-out students that decided her. She said to her employer the next afternoon, when he had finished his playback and she was ostensibly dusting a table in his study, "Do those tapes last?" Except when guests were present she had dropped the "sir" insensibly; her deferential tone implied it. "It would be a shame if anything happened to them, and you had no record."

"Oh, they last. For as long as I'll want them," said Mr. Tomlinson briskly, and Celia made no reply except to whisk her cloth assiduously over the covered and ancient typewriter on a stand in one corner. Something used by his long-dead wife, she wondered, or a trophy from some distant office?

Mr. Tomlinson was preoccupied at dinner. In the morning, he folded his napkin as Celia was clearing the breakfast dishes away and said with shyness, "I don't suppose you type, Celia?"

"I'm afraid not. I took it in high school," said Celia carelessly, waggling her agile fingers which had never touched a keyboard, "but I've forgotten all I ever knew. It's something you have to keep practicing at—there are all kinds of exercises," she added in case she should be invited to sit down there and then.

In a zeal he thought to be entirely his own, Mr. Tomlinson pursued her into the kitchen, an area he usually left austerely to women. "But if you've had the rudiments, it wouldn't be quite like starting from scratch, surely. You'd be able to more or less brush up, wouldn't you? I wonder if there's a place in town that offers courses?"

Fennimore Business School, Celia wanted to say sharply, but she only glanced at him noncommittally as she slid his breakfast dishes gently into hot water and suds.

"It has occurred to me that it might be wise to have a written record," said Mr. Tomlinson, "because that way, if it seemed like a good idea, I could always have a few copies printed and send them to old friends in other parts of the country." He tugged excitedly at his vest. "Would you make some inquiries for me, Celia? I'm not very good on the telephone."

It was a dignified understatement; he could not hear a single transmitted word. Celia finished the dishes, to drive home the impression that any eagerness over this project was on the part of her employer, before she dried her hands and went to consult the telephone book. She informed Mr. Tomlinson presently that the Fennimore Business School had evening classes on Tuesdays and Thursdays, and told him the fee.

It didn't seem to take him aback in the least, afire as

he already was with the notion of a manuscript. "But it would mean giving up your time on those evenings."

"Well . . . I wouldn't mind that. But—I know it's none of my business, but do you think Mrs. Cannon . . . ?"

It had the expected effect. "I am naturally very fond of my niece. However," said Mr. Tomlinson magnificently, "she is not my arbiter. Would you make the necessary arrangements?"

Celia's hands were as deft at a typewriter as they had been at Mrs. Stevenson's sewing machine, and after the first two bewildering sessions she was able to take a look at her fellow students. Except for a few obviously expectant young wives she could not place them with any accuracy, but she knew intuitively that they had nothing to give her. She knew too that theirs was a world which would never impinge on that of Mrs. Cannon or Mr. Tomlinson, and when a blond young man with a wavy profile invited her to have a drink after class she accepted.

His name was Willis Lambert, and he told her over a Tom Collins in a smokily lit lounge that he was a trainee for Temple Insurance; he hoped to be a claims investigator, and although there was no official policy, the company worked you up that much faster if you took any outside courses on your own. This little exposition was followed by an expectant pause, which Celia filled by taking a sip of her drink. Her lowered gaze caught the edge of Willis Lambert's dashingly checked coat sleeve and the massive gold ring with a tiny speck of diamond on his little finger. It was a near-certainty that Willis Lambert would have nothing further to do with anyone in domestic service.

23

"Actually," said Celia—this was a word Hugh Stevenson's girls had used a great deal, and it gave her confidence—"I'm not doing anything at the moment, just sort of looking around." She took refuge in another remembered pause-filler, lifting a hand to trace her already smooth coil of ashy hair. "But typing ought to be good training for something."

"It comes in real handy in an office," agreed Willis Lambert with an appreciative grin. He tapped her glass. "Finish that and we'll have another to relax the old finger muscles."

"Thank you, but I can't, I'm late now," said Celia, feeling a rush of resentment at Mr. Tomlinson and his clock-watching friend who came to play backgammon on her evenings off.

"See you Thursday night," said Willis on the sidewalk, and the interlude after class was plainly included.

Mr. Tomlinson's impatience to commence on what he had begun to call his book grew in direct proportion to Celia's progress at the typewriter—he had had the ancient machine cleaned and to her surprise it actually worked—and her job, and her position in the house, underwent a subtle change. The first manifestation of this was Mr. Tomlinson's decision to have Mrs. Meggs come three days a week instead of two, in order to allow Celia more time at the table in his study. And, like a bat operating on radar, Hester Cannon descended.

She greeted Celia at the door with a cool and raking glance and went directly to her uncle, predictably on his balcony with his field glasses at this hour. She was downstairs again half an hour later with an unaccustomed flush under her yellow eyes and a voice clasped in ice. "Isn't it

24

fortunate for you, Celia, that my uncle is underwriting your secretarial education. I understand that Mrs. Meggs benefits, too. I hope Dr. Fowler is aware of all this excitement?"

Celia gave her a level glance, far removed from the demurely dropped lashes of six months ago. She said with no hint of triumph, because the triumph would come more absolutely from the doctor's own lips, "Yes, he is, Mrs. Cannon."

"Oh? I believe I'll just have a talk with him," said Mrs. Cannon. "It's possible that Dr. Fowler is getting past his abilities . . . I believe I had an umbrella?"

When the door had closed behind her, Celia went about her work unperturbed. Mr. Tomlinson was probably one of the few people left in the country who still had an attendant physician, and Dr. Fowler, who came ceremoniously once every two weeks to check up on the friend whose ills he had diagnosed and treated for fifteen years, was warmly congratulatory toward Celia. Enthusiasm for a project, he told her, was a far more powerful drug than any yet invented by medical science, and he was delighted at the increase in his patient's usually peckish appetite, lack of digestive complaints, and sound sleep without pills. Keep up the good work, Celia.

For the time being, no more was heard from Mrs. Cannon. Mr. Tomlinson did not mention his niece's angry visit, but his unruffled resuming of work in the study the next morning—"Let me see, where were we?"—made a pact between him and Celia. The pact was further sealed on a night in late December.

Willis Lambert had been absent from the typing class, and Celia returned to Stedman Circle earlier than usual.

When she let herself in with her key, shivering from a last attack of snowy wind, it was not two male voices that she heard from the living room, but one male and one female. Before she had quite absorbed this fact she was face to face in the doorway with a handsome gray-haired woman of about sixty, about whose shoulders Mr. Tomlinson was tenderly placing a black coat. Taken aback, but always punctilious, he said, "Eleanor, this is Miss Brett. I've told you what a help she's being. Celia, this is Mrs. Ellwell, a very dear friend of mine."

The two housekeepers, one current, one former, smiled and acknowledged each other. Celia proceeded to the kitchen, where she put away the cheese and crackers left out for the backgammon friend, washed two glasses that had surely contained port, put those away. Darkening the kitchen again, she met Mr. Tomlinson in the lower hall. A listener would have heard only, "Good night, Celia. Class go well?" and "Yes, thank you. Good night." It would have taken a watcher, and a close one at that, to record the glance of complicity that passed between them.

Her employer's choice of companions was a matter of indifference to Celia, but it was a positive pleasure to see Mrs. Cannon outwitted. More importantly, she felt that she need no longer observe her own curfew so carefully. Willis Lambert recovered from his flu, and he and Celia were gradually joined by another couple at their now well-established drink after class. Ted Vanney was an unassuming boy with an easy flush and a bad skin; Betty Schirm had prominent blue eyes, forbidding black brows, and cruelly red lipstick.

She was hostile to Celia from the first, perhaps because she had measured Ted against Willis and decided to make a change. She said when the waiter had trudged away with the drink order, "Funny I haven't seen you around before this."

"You probably have, and didn't notice."

"No, I'd remember," said Betty Schirm, studying Celia with secret-police authority. "Do you have one of those new bachelor-girl apartments near the school?"

Celia had known this would come, sometime. "I don't have an apartment, I live at home."

"Really?" Betty Schirm managed to invest the single word with surprise and mild contempt. She also had the air of someone who was going to look up all the Bretts in the telephone book at the earliest opportunity. "Your house must be fairly nearby, then, as I notice you don't take the subway."

"It's not too far," said Celia with calm, but she took the image of that bright, bullying blue gaze back to Stedman Circle with her that night. She had no illusions about what would happen if Willis learned in what capacity she worked for Mr. Tomlinson. She would either have to drop out of the after-class gatherings, or . . .

Mr. Tomlinson solved the problem for her by catching a cold.

For the first time since she had known him, Celia brought his bourbon and water, and later his dinner, up to his room on a tray. When she went downstairs again the house seemed peculiarly her own: no dry little cough, no rustle of the evening newspaper, no possibility of immediate summons. Without actually planning it, she set the dining room table as she set it for her employer and had her dinner there; the thought crossed her mind that anyone entering might easily assume that she was dining

27

alone because her old . . . uncle was sick.

Mr. Tomlinson was up and about the next day, but that did not alter Celia's intentions. She had alarmed Mrs. Stevenson into finding her another job and she had changed her last name, but she had acted out of inadvertence in the first case and impulse in the second.

What she was to do now would be very deliberate indeed.

Four

Celia usually did an hour's work in the study with Mr. Tomlinson at ten A.M., when the kitchen had been set in order and the day's marketing done by telephone. She put in another hour at four, but chose the morning for her purpose as her employer was then at his best: pink, as yet untired, hand-rubbingly eager to see a few more pages of his irrelevancies in black and white.

She said directly, "Mr. Tomlinson, if it's all right with you I'd like to have a few of my friends in after class tonight."

Mr. Tomlinson gazed at her in puzzled disbelief and cupped an ear. "A few of your . . . ?" It was clear that he thought his hearing to be at fault, and Celia's resolve hardened.

"A few of my friends," she repeated levelly, "as I can only see my family once a month." Then, so that there should be no misunderstanding, she added, "We wouldn't be here until nine thirty. I could see you settled comfortably upstairs before I go. Or if Mrs. Ellwell will be coming in—"

The courteous old blue eyes gazed steadily back, understanding perfectly, weighing Celia's undeniable competence and protection from his niece in the matter of Mrs. Ellwell against the indignity of being forced upstairs in his own house before nine thirty. The gaze also comprehended the sheet of paper she had wheeled into the old typewriter, over whose keyboard her fingers were poised as though they might never fall again.

"That will be quite all right, Celia," said Mr. Tomlinson. "I'll be able to manage very well by myself. Nine thirty, you say? Now, I believe we left off with that tape where I met the young fellow . . ."

Celia was taking a risk, she knew, but a minimal one. Dr. Fowler's calls were in the afternoon, at stated intervals, and out of deference to Mr. Tomlinson's age there were no unscheduled evening droppers-in. Mrs. Cannon had been on the telephone the morning before in her crisp weekly interrogation; it was very unlikely that, living in Manhattan with her stockbroker husband, she would undertake a visit to New Jersey at night.

Still, Celia felt a qualm as she stood on the frost-twinkled sidewalk after the typing class that night and suggested that they all go back to her house for a change. She was casual about it, as though she didn't care either way, and she mentioned in an offhand tone that they would have to be on the quiet side as her uncle was having one of his bad spells, but at bottom there was a terrible thought: What if the old man had changed his mind, and was sitting in the living room in his quiet anger when they came trooping in?

Her apprehension was only increased by the fact that Betty Schirm and Ted Vanney and Willis were all impressed by the mere mention of Stedman Circle; although the house was old-fashioned it was apparently a very good address. Willis, beside Celia in the back seat of Ted's surprisingly new car, gave her a proud possessive squeeze. If after all this . . . ?

But it went off without a hitch. The house, seen by Celia with new eyes, held only the faint lemony scent of the furniture polish favored by Mrs. Meggs and an unmistakable air of tenancy somewhere above. She put a cautionary finger to her lips to remind them all of it, closed the living room door, and stopped worrying.

The evening was an unqualified success. Mr. Tomlinson kept an ample variety of liquor for his guests, but Celia had punctiliously supplied her own along with nuts and potato chips. Going unerringly for napkins and glasses and ice, she seemed indeed a niece of the house. In the unfamiliar atmosphere of old brocade chairs and parchment-shaded lamps and an entire wall of books with polished bindings, Ted Vanney was apprehensive, Betty Schirm awed and envious, Willis complacent. Celia herself, who had started reading the society pages when she worked at the Strykers', felt like a debutante at her coming-out party. When she had closed the front door after them at shortly before midnight, she stood unmoving in the hall for a few moments before she commenced the process of cleaning up.

Her whole body felt as her face once had when she had tried the beaten-egg-white treatment recommended by a magazine—curiously tight and new and invulnerable. It was just as well that there were all those nut dishes and

31

ashtrays and glasses to be dealt with, as she could not possibly have slept yet. Willis Lambert had actually sat in Mr. Tomlinson's wing chair, she had occupied the one facing it, Betty Schirm and Ted Vanney had taken the dark-blue velvet couch. In her odd excitement Celia now dropped down into each place, studying the room from different perspectives, seeing this background as they must have seen it.

A growing awareness of Willis's cigar haze brought her to her feet. She opened a window, unbothered by the rushing cold—in this mood no physical discomfort could touch her—but closed it when, almost at once, the oil burner burst into its dim roar. She sprayed air freshener about instead. Half an hour later, kitchen immaculate for the morning, she was in bed.

She told the dark ceiling that that was that; she had simply taken a single and necessary step to avert what had threatened to become a crisis. The question of having her friends in again need not come up, but if it did she would say regretfully that her uncle was very much worse, and the doctor had said absolutely no visitors in the house . . .

. . . Wouldn't she?

Mr. Tomlinson was his usual decorous self in the morning. He did not refer in any way to the evening before—although he could hardly have forgotten, the alien cigar smoke having triumphed heavily over the air freshener—and neither did Celia, who had been prepared to thank him prettily. Two years ago such a silence, such a complete wiping-out of an astonishing departure, would have struck her as menacing, and indeed from the Strykers it would have been, but she had learned that people like Mr. Tomlinson reduced possibly awkward situations to nothingness by ignoring them.

In March, something happened which would prove to be of the utmost importance to Celia. Mrs. Ellwell died of pneumonia.

Mr. Tomlinson, more than twenty years her senior, was stunned with grief and incredulity. There was no question of his attending the funeral, as it was in Hampstead where her late husband was buried, but it was Celia who went personally to order his flowers and return to tell her employer that they were beautiful, exactly what he had specified. It was Celia who suggested that Mrs. Ellwell would have liked him to finish his book and gradually joggled him back to life again.

Dr. Fowler said that for a few days there it had been nip and tuck. Mrs. Cannon, who had never bothered to learn the names of the various threats to her inheritance, went unaware and said nothing at all until it was too late and her uncle, usually so gentle of tongue, turned on her with such vehemence that she sought Celia out angrily in the kitchen.

"Really, Celia, you might have let me know about Mrs. Ellwell. Although why it could have been such a shock . . . he can't have seen the woman for months and months—"

This time Celia did keep her lashes down. She said quietly and with some degree of truth that although she did not have Mrs. Cannon's telephone number Dr. Fowler did, and had assured her that if his patient became critical at any time he would let Mrs. Cannon know. She did not add that in her opinion Dr. Fowler, not pleased at his last interview with Mrs. Cannon, would leave that very late.

Mrs. Cannon paced handsomely. She was too proud to

appear suddenly as the loving niece whose sole concern was her uncle's happiness, but she said sharply, "I understand that you've been very helpful, Celia, but in the future—here, I'll give you my telephone number—I would appreciate your letting me know if anything like this happens again. You needn't wait," she added wintrily, "until Dr. Fowler decides it's necessary."

Celia thought later that it might have been that day when Mr. Tomlinson made up his mind—but of course she knew nothing about it at the time.

What did become apparent was a favorable shift in her own situation. Until Mrs. Ellwell's death Mr. Tomlinson had enjoyed, however surreptitiously, the best of both worlds: Celia to run his house and do his typing by day, his portly forbidden flame to spend a few hours with him on an occasional evening. He came of an unbending generation and would not have heard a word uttered against his niece in his presence, but he would never have turned to Mrs. Cannon for comfort.

Perhaps unaware that he was doing so, he turned to Celia.

The process came about so gradually that even Mrs. Meggs, on the scene three days a week, would only be able to shake her head dumbly at official questions later. To Dr. Fowler, Celia remained the self-possessed young woman who had cooperated with him at every turn and almost certainly prolonged his patient's life. To the infrequent visitors, she was notable chiefly for her baked clams.

She slid out of uniform imperceptibly; it would have been hard to say where the charcoal wool-and-acetate ordered by Mrs. Cannon ended and the lighter gray or taupe began. The simple lines stayed much the same because they became her—with her bold shoulders she would never be able to wear floaty or frilly clothes—and took kindly, on her evenings off, to the chunky costume jewelry then in fashion.

In his first access of grief over Mrs. Ellwell's death Mr. Tomlinson said bewilderedly, "It seems so strange that she should go, while I . . . Don't leave me, Celia."

"I won't, Mr. Tomlinson. Not now," said Celia, and the implied deadline agitated him almost as much as if she had given notice on the spot; he forgot that ten months ago Celia had been the interloper supplanting Mrs. Ellwell. "Aren't you happy here, Celia? If it's a matter of salary . . ."

Celia was far too shrewd to give up her present advantages for the sake of a few extra dollars a week and eventual dismissal; if Mrs. Cannon had managed to have her way about Mrs. Ellwell she would certainly have her way about Celia. So she said that although she was satisfied with her salary this was a lonely situation for someone her age, seeing her family only once a month as she did.

"But you have friends," pointed out Mr. Tomlinson. "The young people you had in one evening."

One evening, Celia's pensive gaze reminded him, and that five weeks ago. She sat at the typewriter with an air of abstracted thought, and as though he feared that this would lead to an unfavorable decision Mr. Tomlinson said hastily, "I'm sure we can arrange something." He gave a deep, premonitory sigh, which he covered at once with an anxious smile and a glance at his pocket watch. "Perhaps that's enough work for this morning. I can't seem to arrange my thoughts . . ."

Celia's determination to repeat that single evening was never far out of her thoughts, but apart from that she was very contented.

Far from objecting to the typing, she found it a pleasant change from purely domestic routine. She was careful not to show any reflection of her increased stature in the house to Mrs. Meggs, and as a result the two got along well. The cleaning woman was pleased at her extra day's work; Celia was equally pleased that her own duties in that area, never arduous, were further cut down.

Nor was she lonely in the sense that she had implied to Mr. Tomlinson. She still saw Willis Lambert once a week, although he was becoming a nuisance after a weekend she had finally consented to spend with him at Fire Island; she was now interested in him as a convenience, a ticket to places where a woman looked odd alone. Ted Vanney and Betty Schirm had vanished into some orbit which contained a bowling league, and, in her growing experience, Celia was not anxious to replace them in kind.

She was saving almost all of her salary, and on the weekends when she supposedly visited her family—Mrs. Cannon and her plump nondescript husband came to stay discontentedly in the guest room on these occasions—she went to New York. Here she wandered the streets and gazed into the windows of stores she knew only from dazzling advertisements; once, at Bonwit Teller's, she bought a four-dollar rope of pearls and carried the distinctive little bag about with her all that day and the next.

And always, as she had from the day she arrived at the Stevensons', she observed. She stayed at an inexpensive hotel and ate at glaringly lit places with smudged plastic-covered menus, and in between she sauntered into the lobbies of good hotels, sat down with the casual attitude of someone meeting a guest there, and drank in her surroundings. As usual, she discarded the men; it was the women she watched. She saw how they arrived at hotels and how, leaving, they met the problem of the bellboy and the doorman. Puzzlingly, the lone women did not have the flustered, self-conscious air Celia connected with such a state; they walked with as much poise as though the hotel had been especially built for them.

She listened to scraps of conversation to take back to Stedman Circle and muse over later: "Well, of course, that was when refugees were smart. Now it's retarded children." "—terribly upset, because after all that he turned out to be Sagittarius and you know what *that* means." "She's dragged that poor man to so many of those Hunt Club affairs that he can't even jog any more. He canters."

When Celia returned to the tall old house at six o'clock on Sunday evening, Mrs. Cannon, almost friendly with the prospect of release, would ask perfunctorily, "Family all well, Celia?" and Celia would reply, "Yes, thank you, Mrs. Cannon."

"Ma'am" had gone forever out of her life.

She was confident that her conversation with her employer in his study would bear fruit, and she was right. When she was removing the remains of his tapioca pudding and coffee that evening, he said, "I've been thinking over what we talked about this morning, Celia. This is a big house for one old man, and I don't see any reason why"—he appeared to have difficulty in swallowing here, but recovered himself —"you shouldn't have a few young people in occasionally. You'd let me know in advance, of course."

So that he could be spirited away upstairs: that was

37

implicit.

"Oh, of course," said Celia, over a leap of exultation so violent that it was almost physically painful. She gave him a level look out of her dark eyes. "It would make such a difference to me, Mr. Tomlinson, but . . . I wouldn't want anyone to think I was taking advantage of you."

Like Mrs. Cannon, said this little pause. Or even friendly Dr. Fowler.

A faint hint of what might have been wryness crept into Mr. Tomlinson's polite old eyes and was gone at once. "I see no reason why our arrangements should concern anyone else at all," he said mildly, and, less than a year after she had first entered it, Celia became quasi-mistress of 4 Stedman Circle. It was a situation with disaster for her inherent in it; she was saved by the native shrewdness that goes hand in hand with personal ambition—that and, early in June, the simple fact of a torn pocketbook lining.

Five

It was not surprising that Celia's occasional entertaining, with her employer notified in advance and firmly kept apart from it, went undetected. Mr. Tomlinson did not know any of his immediate neighbors—it was a long time since he had ventured out of his own front door—but he was not a recluse, and cars parked in front of No. 4 might, with its narrow frontage, have been overflows from No. 2 or No. 6 in any case.

Dr. Fowler's professional calls were never in the evening, and Celia was in command of the telephone; she could always tell a caller, if she had plans of her own, that Mr. Tomlinson had retired for the night. Her habit of cleaning living room and kitchen before going to bed was so ingrained by years of service as a maid that Mrs. Meggs was none the wiser, and if Mrs. Cannon had any spies in Stedman Circle, they slept.

Celia was modest with her guest list, out of necessity. There was Willis, and Willis's cousin and his wife on a visit from Arkansas, and a couple from a nearby town who were friends of the cousin. These new additions, who might have tended to be raucous in other surroundings, were muted almost to dumbness by the lemony, camphory elegance of the house. They looked upon Willis with respect as the future husband of the heir to all this, a fact of which Celia grew sharply and unpleasantly aware.

She had no intention of marrying Willis; in her trips to New York and her observations there, she had far outgrown his wavy profile and elbow nudges and ridiculous ring. She would have to do something, but in the meantime she was caught in a trap of her own devising. She would not have hesitated now to identify her lofty position ("Poor old soul, I had to promise that I wouldn't leave him") but the die was cast there and it would not do to have conflicting stories in a town as small as this.

It was certainly true that, in a manner that only a psychiatrist might have unraveled, Mr. Tomlinson had grown to love his chains. But there were sounder reasons too for his willing thralldom: Celia fixed his meals exactly as he liked them and knew to the minute how long he could stand a visit from his old friend Mrs. Holt, who was even deafer than he. No plate or glass or ornament ever got broken. Most important of all, Celia had finished a complete rough typing of what he called his book, and on which he was now beginning to make excited little revisions with a fountain pen.

He could talk to Celia about Mrs. Ellwell, and always receive a sympathetic response. ("I could tell she was a lovely woman.") It was a small sacrifice to go very early to bed perhaps once in two weeks, and although he loathed the smell of cigar smoke, it did not linger so much now that it was late May, and the windows could be open in the

40

evening.

On the afternoon of the thirty-first, when Mr. Tomlinson was alternately reading and bird watching on his balcony, Celia heard her name cried dimly and urgently. She had been putting away a delivery of groceries, and cans scattered and fell as she ran up the stairs and into Mr. Tomlinson's bedroom. He was there, braced against the edge of the outer doorway, his face candle-colored, his breath coming in great, slow, deliberate swells. Out of one of these he managed, "Dizzy . . . help me . . . bed."

Celia supported him strongly to his bed, instinctively hooking one arm about her own broad shoulder. He lay there for a few minutes with his head back and his fragile eyelids closed and trembling; his breath still came in that effortful way, and Celia was too frightened to speak and perhaps interrupt it. Only when his lids lifted and he said with surprising strength, "Thank you, Celia," did she dare to move, to say, "Will you be all right for a minute? I'll call Dr. Fowler."

"No need. A moment's dizziness, that's all," said Mr. Tomlinson, but of course he had not seen himself and Celia, backing toward the door, tried frantically to recall what she had heard or read about such seizures. "Can I get you some water? Or brandy?"

Mr. Tomlinson, eyes closed again, nodded slightly to one or the other, and Celia fled down the stairs and telephoned Dr. Fowler.

At the doctor's proposal of removal to the hospital, a cardiograph and a period of observation, Mr. Tomlinson, by now sitting up in a chair with his normal pinkness restored, was courteously immovable. He was convinced that he would not emerge from a hospital alive, and although

41

Dr. Fowler said nonsense, he was privately inclined to agree. He had often seen it happen with very elderly people: somehow the public admission that there was something seriously wrong, and the mere fact of being clinically watched, had all the inevitability of a balloon and a pin. It was entirely possible that if he were taken away from his birds and his beloved manuscript Mr. Tomlinson would quietly give up.

"Well, at least do something about the stairs," said Fowler when the patient further refused to have his first-floor study converted into a bedroom. "I don't say you'll have another of these attacks—there's a good chance you may not—but there ought to be a handrail along the wall just in case. And I'd stay away from that balcony if I were you."

Mr. Tomlinson was in heartfelt agreement, as it was on the balcony that the vertigo had seized him. The next day the handrail was installed against the inner wall of the stairway; the sight of it made Celia apprehensive, but it was apparently to be the only reminder of Mr. Tomlinson's frightening attack.

She called Mrs. Cannon to report this event, not from any sense of duty but out of a strong suspicion that Dr. Fowler would and it might be just as well to be ahead of him. "He ought to be in a hospital," said Mrs. Cannon at once; her voice seemed to hold an anticipatory note. But then a fast calculation of hospital expenses evidently seized her, because she added hastily, "Or whatever Dr. Fowler thinks."

As this was not in Celia's domain, she only said, "I was sure you'd want to know," and was thanked crisply. The entire conversation had not lasted for more than three minutes, but it was one on which Celia would look back gratefully.

On a June day thundery with heat, with Dr. Fowler expected, Celia went to the study to get her employer's library list as usual. Her pocketbook was already on the hall table. She started to tuck the list into the side compartment, remembered the tear in the lining down which it had vanished the week before, and laid it down on the table; it would be far more accessible in a dress pocket than in the jumble of the bag's main interior.

She waited as always to let the doctor in, smiled and said that Mr. Tomlinson seemed almost his old self, and went upstairs to change her dress; she never, now, went into town in even semiuniform. She had gone three of the six blocks to the library before she stopped short, thrust a hand into her pocket, turned resignedly.

She had left the list on the hall table, and had not even glanced at its contents. Not just anything would do for Mr. Tomlinson; he had what Celia considered a strange taste for nonfiction, with perhaps a mystery novel or two for mitigation. She would have to go back.

She let herself into the house with great care. She had no idea of what Dr. Fowler did on these occasions, but had a dim and almost superstitious feeling that they were somehow sacred. She tiptoed to the hall table, picked up the list, heard the voices from the study, heard her own name.

"—to Celia. Hester would only sell it, and she and her husband certainly don't need the money. Celia's been very good to me, you know. I could never have gotten my book done without her. In fact, I'd never have thought of it—you'll get the first copy, by the way. She's really a very unusual young woman."

"Oh, I agree thoroughly." This was Dr. Fowler. "She's undoubtedly deserving, but have you given a thought to skyrocketing real-estate prices, Bob? This place is worth a good deal. Your niece may not unnaturally—"

"It's done." Mr. Tomlinson, in one of his rare flashes of autocracy. "I'm only telling you so that you can certify, if it should ever become necessary, that it was done in my right mind. You *would* certify to that, I trust?"

Snort of laughter from Dr. Fowler. "No question about that. Now, let's get the shirt off . . ."

Celia let herself out with a housebreaker's stealth, waiting to ease the door shut until the voices had resumed again. Although her blood was hammering wildly in her head, some kind of automatic pilot observed coolly that she had better get to the library in half the usual time, so that she could find Mr. Tomlinson's selections and return as punctually as though she had never made that trip back and never heard—never heard . . .

At the library desk, she almost stammered. She had been coming here for nearly a year, but suddenly the rental-book stand, the dry hush, the librarian's earnest face (Mrs. Ohm, she was), the cut-out and pasted daisies surrounding a notice that there would be a children's story hour on Saturday, the menacing little notice under glass about fines for book damage (dog bites were fifteen cents) seemed as alien as the features of a land visited in a dream.

("This place is worth a good deal." "It's done.")

She tried to shake off the trancelike state as she returned at speed; for all she knew, Dr. Fowler might have powers of divination. But she took an objective view of 4 Sted-

44

man Circle—hers!—as she approached it, and was able, because of the oppressive, purple-clouded heat, to pass a handkerchief quite naturally over her forehead as she said in the study, "The book on falconry was out, sir, but I got everything else."

"Thank you, Celia," said Mr. Tomlinson in exactly his usual tone, and it would have needed preknowledge to detect a slightly more personal interest in Dr. Fowler's bright gray eyes. Celia willed her own knowledge to erase itself, although it felt like a birthmark. She asked composedly if they would care for iced coffee or tea, was told no, and retreated to the kitchen.

Her kitchen, ultimately. Given a man of eighty-three, soon.

But, as though the mere revising of his will had lent him new vigor, Mr. Tomlinson throve. A footnote in his manuscript said that his mother had lived to be eighty-nine, his father ninety-two. Celia had read in a syndicated medical-advice column that, barring accident or acute infection, you were apt to live approximately as long as your parents.

Discontent came slowly at first, not assuaged by Dr. Fowler's jocular, "Marvelous, isn't he? He may bury us all," and was followed by impatience. Celia was like a child who, discovering Christmas, starts to wonder, How many days? How many, indeed? Mr. Tomlinson began to seem to her like an hourglass with an obstacle in the middle, preventing the final flow.

Meanwhile, it was essential that there be no change in her own demeanor, although they would not be looking for one as she had presumably been at the library when that all-important conversation took place. Nevertheless, Celia was careful not to be sweeter tempered than usual with her employer, especially in the presence of Dr. Fowler. She watched her step on Mrs. Cannon's rare visits, and her friendly fellow-employee relationship with Mrs. Meggs went unchanged.

As she would have no future use for, or need of, Willis Lambert, Celia set about discouraging him, but in Willis's world this was a standard feminine ploy and his ardor redoubled. She breathed a sigh of relief when Temple Insurance dispatched him to their home office in Milwaukee for further training.

"We could be married first," suggested Willis eagerly and covetously, "and I could send for you."

"That wouldn't be fair to you *or* the company," said Celia firmly. "They think they're getting a single man, you know," and Willis gave her a last nudge with his elbow and was gone.

In her room at night she studied the real-estate columns in the evening paper, and on her day off she went to look at some of the houses that seemed to resemble 4 Stedman Circle in size, neighborhood, and facilities. She discovered that, with the commercial area gnawing steadily away at the fringes of the good residential area, Mr. Tomlinson's back garden was a considerable asset. She finally arrived at an approximate figure of fifty-five thousand dollars.

Eventually. *And* if Mr. Tomlinson did not change his mind for some reason. As he had the invincible stubbornness which often accompanies a mild disposition, conventionality seemed to pose the worst threat, although he had certainly been unconventional enough in the matter of Mrs. Ellwell. That lady's demise appeared to have put blinders on Mrs. Cannon; she made her duty visits to her uncle, and no more.

46

At eight thirty on the morning of June fourteenth, having finished her own breakfast of boiled egg and dry toast and coffee, Celia began the preparation of Mr. Tomlinson's oatmeal. He was as severe about the easy five-minute kind as he was about tea bags, and she had put on the kettle for the scalding of the teapot and was placing his egg on the counter when she heard her name called once more in that distant and terrified way.

She did not run, this time. She steadied the egg in its precipitate roll (no point in having to clean *that* up, when the frantic summons would turn out as it had before) and lodged it securely behind the readied cup and saucer. Then she mounted the stairs and went into Mr. Tomlinson's bedroom, hearing "Celia!" in a diminishing voice three more times on the way. She did not answer.

The door to the forbidden balcony stood wide, moving a little in the breeze. At the base of one of the upright iron bars was Mr. Tomlinson's desperate old hand, hanging on somehow, and from the space below came Mr. Tomlinson's desperate old voice: "Celia! Help me!"

Celia was immensely strong, and his weight was a fragile one. She could have leaned over the balcony railing and tried to lift him, or at least secured him a firmer grip. She could have called, "Hold on, I'm going for help!" and raced down the stairs, shrieked at the top of her lungs on the sidewalk, sped around to the garden and managed to break his fall.

She stood very still among the brown broadloom, thrown-back white candlewick, old-fashioned dresser and photographs which marked Mr. Tomlinson's private precincts. She had been here often before, of course, making the bed and dusting, but now she took careful note of the framed bird pictures on the walls—the one of the black-and-yellow hen in which nestlings could be seen if you looked closely, and the glowing watercolor of massed canvasbacks at evening, with no set of down-sweeping wings the same.

An echo said somewhere, "It's done." But it seemed an eternity, when she took her gaze away from the walls, before the ivory-knuckled hand slipped almost wispily from its grip on the iron railing. It took so long that there were small dark-red crescents on the cushions of Celia's thumbs where her nails had bitten.

After a muffled sound of impact on the square of concrete below, there was total silence. The house was full of the smell of burning oatmeal.

Six

When the contents of the will became known, Mrs. Cannon demanded an autopsy. As her timing showed only greed and vindictiveness—she had been quite content with accident until she learned of her uncle's bequest to his housekeeper—and as the police surgeon and the hospital were in full agreement with Dr. Fowler as to the cause of death, this was denied.

For, although after a lightning glance at Mr. Tomlinson's bonelessly crumpled form Celia had assumed it safe to telephone Dr. Fowler at once, Mr. Tomlinson wasn't quite dead. True to his parentage, he had lived for six hours, unconscious, in the intensive-care unit of the nearest hospital. Celia stayed in the waiting room until Mrs. Cannon arrived, her total pallor appearing to reflect horror—as it did. At any time the old man might wake and mutter what must be uttermost in his appalled brain: "I kept calling Celia, and I heard her come"—like all the deaf he was hypersensitive to vibration—"and she wouldn't answer me."

But he did not wake. Along with his neatly folded clothes in the hospital room where he died of deep shock were the field glasses which had been removed from around his neck, a mute statement of how he had come to be on the balcony at all.

So much for the actual cause of death, but what had immediately preceded it? Somewhat stiffly, in view of the rather unusual circumstances and Mrs. Cannon's deadly perserverance, an inquest was granted. From it emerged Mr. Tomlinson's earlier attack of dizziness, the lack of a single mark on his body that would not have been occasioned by his fall, and Dr. Fowler's firm conviction that Celia had had absolutely no previous knowledge that she would benefit under the will. "Mr. Tomlinson told me of his intention in confidence."

He was asked alertly, "Why was that, Doctor?"

Dr. Fowler's sharp gaze did not go anywhere near Mrs. Cannon's yellow eye as he said austerely, "I had been Robert Tomlinson's friend as well as his physician for fifteen years."

The reekingly burned breakfast, evocative of a housekeeper hurrying in response to a cry of distress or alarm, seemed to speak for itself, particularly in view of Celia's frantic summons of Dr. Fowler on the occasion of his earlier attack. Mrs. Meggs, who had worked at the house far longer than Celia and not been mentioned in the will at all, carried unobtrusive weight when, asked if it was her impression that the housekeeper knew of any expectations, she shook her varnish-brown head. "She never said anything to me. Well, I guess she wouldn't anyway, but it stands to reason that she would have changed, sort of, doesn't it?"

The verdict of accidental death, a moral certainty ahead of time, now became official. Mrs. Cannon stopped Celia in the tan-painted corridor outside. She wore black with a twist of gray chiffon at the throat and an expression of cold amazement that, a year ago, she had actually sought out Celia in a guest bedroom at the Strykers' and invited her into this costly fringe of her life.

For the first time, openly, they were not semiemployer and servant but two well-matched feminine antagonists. Mrs. Cannon said in a low and bladelike voice, "I don't know how you managed it, but I will never believe that you didn't have a hand in my uncle's death. I'll contest the will, of course."

Celia, in a subdued taupe dress with white collar and cuffs, tipped her head briefly in a way that did not quite say, Go ahead and try it. What she said aloud, with the conviction of perfect truth was, "I'm sorry, Mrs. Cannon. I don't know how to convince you, but I never laid a finger on Mr. Tomlinson."

And she hadn't.

She spent the night at 4 Stedman Circle, because nobody had cautioned her not to, and walked through its rooms like a very young girl in a dream. Downstairs, the kitchen, lavatory, dining room, living room, study; upstairs, guest room and bath, her own room which now looked shabby and shrunken, Mr. Tomlinson's bath and bedroom, mysteriously restored by Mrs. Meggs so that it bore no trace of his violent departure from it. A steep little flight of stairs led to an attic, but Celia did not go there.

She paused in her tour and looked at herself in mirrors as she passed them, and in some manner her reflection within the various frames, against the various back-grounds, made the house hers more securely than any number of documents. She was not really worried about Mrs. Cannon's threat of contesting the will; she was confident that Dr. Fowler would crush firmly any suggestion that Mr. Tomlinson had been of unsound mind when he made it.

On the other hand, Celia would be just as pleased if no rumor of her activities as hostess got back to Mrs. Cannon's ears. She had an uneasy feeling that a lawyer might be able to make something unpleasant out of that. The danger seemed diminished by the fact that although the evening paper had carried a small paragraph about the inquest, a narcotics raid in Newark and a local bank robbery had driven it onto an inside page. It would have to be read in its entirety, moreover; Celia had always said merely, "my uncle." It was unlikely that any one of that handful of people would pursue the obsequies of Robert E. Tomlinson, aged 83.

Willis Lambert was safely in Milwaukee, his cousin and wife had returned to Arkansas. Somewhere, presumably, there remained Betty Schirm, but Celia would cross that bridge when she came to it.

She turned out the lights and went to bed in her own small room, hugging the thought that she could just as easily have slept in the guest room, where she had changed the linen herself after the Cannons' last visit. It was perhaps a comprehensive summing-up that no vision of an old hand wrapped frantically around a railing bar entered her dreams at all.

Advised by her lawyer, who talked to Dr. Fowler and sent out a few discreet feelers among Mr. Tomlinson's friends, Mrs. Cannon did not contest the will, but the cost to her temper was high. It showed on an afternoon in late September when, by prearrangement, she came to 4 Stedman Circle to collect her uncle's personal effects.

Although the will had stipulated that Celia be allowed immediate occupancy, she had not stayed at the house after the first few days. When the novelty of this domain had worn off, she felt exposed—to exactly what, she could not have said. She had none of the resources of a person solitary by nature, and yet, going out, she did not care for being an object of mild interest. She had also begun to receive eager letters from Willis, announcing that he would be home in December and "Will this call for a celebration!!!"

Even in his absence Willis was as annoying to Celia as a partially dangling hem. It seemed expedient to be thoroughly gone from the scene by the time he returned, although in a thoughtful way that would have gratified him she kept his letters, and she consulted Dr. Fowler, who was a coexecutor, about closing up the house until the time of probate. "It doesn't feel—right, somehow, my living there."

In his way Dr. Fowler was almost as old-fashioned as Mr. Tomlinson, and this humble sentiment appealed to him. He suggested that she air the house now and then and advise the police that it would be vacant. Celia agreed to both, packed her bags, and removed herself to a rather shabby but respectable New York hotel to consider her future. The drain on her savings worried her, idle as she was for the first time in her adult life, but she had an almost superstitious conviction that whatever she did next would be of immense importance for good or ill.

She had still not come to a decision on the afternoon

when there was a crisp clicking sound at the front door—no one had had the temerity to ask Mrs. Cannon for her key—and, moments later, Mrs. Cannon's black head poked inquiringly around the living room doorway. At the sight of Celia rising without hurry, open magazine in hand, she said "Oh, quite at home!" in a tone an uninitiate might have thought congratulatory. She indicated the suitcase in one gloved hand. "Perhaps you'd like to come up with me to see what I take?"

The nature of the invitation was lost on the usually acute Celia. She said deprecatingly, "Oh, I know that isn't necessary," and the earnestness stung Mrs. Cannon far more thoroughly than any amount of mockery. She proceeded upstairs at a pace which miraculously did not leave little round holes in the carpeting.

Celia returned to her magazine. She had a fairly accurate idea of what Mrs. Cannon would want in the way of personal effects: a surprising amount of men's jewelry in a leather case, photograph frames which Mr. Tomlinson had once told her were platinum, a valuable camera with which, until his sight had begun to deteriorate, he had photographed birds in his garden. Even in her acquisitiveness she would hardly claim the wealth of old-fashioned suits and coats. Besides, there wasn't room in the suitcase.

Celia was up and strolling about when her visitor descended and turned toward the study, saying edgedly over her emerald wool shoulder ". . . Well. You've certainly come up in the world, haven't you, Celia?"

"Yes, I have, Mrs. Cannon," replied Celia with dangerous humility.

"I don't imagine"—Mrs. Cannon was now almost absentmindedly stowing into the suitcase a presentation gold-and-onyx penholder, an antique letter-opener, a paper-weight of some curious, glinting stone— "that you'll be looking for any more situations now, will you?"

Celia had the kind of smooth heavy skin that almost never betrayed the color of rage, and it did not now. She said, "I don't know yet what my plans are," and then, although nature had left her without a sense of humor in the same random way it had presented her with an impressive bone structure, she walked to the typewriter table. Deftly, she stuffed a great mass of annotated typescript into an outsize brown envelope, twirled the cord to close it, thrust it at Mrs. Cannon. "I know Mr. Tomlinson would have wanted you to have this," she said seriously. "It's his book."

The suddenness of the gesture caught Mrs. Cannon by surprise, and she was clasping the bulky envelope before she knew it. She stared at Celia with a flash of ice in her yellow eyes as awareness dawned, and then, unexpectedly, she threw back her black head and laughed with a touch of wildness.

"You're sharp, I'll give you that," she said, and snapped the suitcase shut, settled the camera more securely over her shoulder and, still holding the envelope, moved out into the hall. "If you wouldn't mind getting the door?"

Celia opened it. Stedman Circle still had trees in spite of encroaching industry, and shadows stirred over the polish of the dark-gray Imperial parked outside. "I won't say goodbye," said Mrs. Cannon to Celia with a curiously menacing head-to-toe smile, "because we never know what might come up, do we? I'll just say . . . no, I won't say that either."

She walked rapidly down the steps, closed herself and her cargo into the car with an expensive thump, and drove away. Celia, gazing after her, puzzled over that last phrase and decided that Mrs. Cannon had toyed with, and discarded, "good luck."

The house was appraised at $56,500, and the real-estate firm engaged by Celia's lawyer—she had been horrified to find that she needed a lawyer—was of the opinion that a buyer would not be hard to find. She was also dismayed to learn that the periodic services of the gardener who kept the rear of 4 Stedman Circle from turning into a weedy jungle were now being charged to her.

Accustomed as she was to room and board, she was astonished at the speed with which money melted away. Breakfasts of tomato juice and coffee, frugal drugstore lunches, the hotel's special for dinner, mounted to what seemed like an astronomical sum. When you did not wear launderable uniforms, clothes and dry cleaning took another bite. City pavements were ruinous to the lifts on heels.

And there was the five dollars—an unvarying sum since Celia had first gone to work at the Stevensons'—that went weekly to her family. She sent it out of wariness rather than any feeling of obligation, because although she had Anglicized her name it was always possible that, if the money stopped, they might trace her somehow and, discovering the legacy, descend upon her like wolves. Celia had not seen any of them for four years, and in fact had only a vague idea of the ages of her younger sisters and brothers, but she was coldly sure that they would want appendixes out, or night school, or wedding garments. The only dream that ever frightened her contained the flaking yellow tenement in Bridgeport and its sponge-like demand for cash.

She would never be reduced to that again. When she got the money from the sale of the house she would buy a few really good clothes and then she would . . . what?

On her first visits to New York she had been awed and dazzled by the sleek, pretty, astonishingly well-dressed girls who poured out of elevators in marble lobbies every afternoon. Now, less awed, she studied them at greater length and knew without regret that theirs was a world in which she could not compete even if she mastered shorthand. They had some indefinable quality which she would never possess—lightheartedness? The confidence instilled by high school dates and college proms and added to ever since? Whatever it was, they were as clustered as birds and as given to carefree, spontaneous cascades of sound.

But for all their wit and intelligence they were, to Celia, in ruts. Smooth and attractive ruts, certainly, but still. She had no idea, as she watched them at Schrafft's, that she had somewhat the air of a puma observing house cats.

She was not yet articulate enough to put her own situation into words, but she had had a taste of power. She had done her real maturing among the extremely well-to-do, if not the actually wealthy, and what she really wanted was to be accepted on their own level by the kind of people for whom she had brought cocktails, pressed evening dresses, peeled small yellow *grapes,* on one unforgettable occasion, for a guest who idly fancied them with rum and powdered sugar. To be, not "Celia" but

57

"There's Celia Brett."

To another girl who less than five years ago had stumbled over her English and painstakingly learned how to set a dinner table, it might have seemed a ridiculous goal. To Celia, waiting for the sale of a house snatched from the jaws of Mrs. Cannon, it did not seem impossible at all.

She took the first step almost by accident.

Seven

Celia's room, one of the cheapest at the Hotel Alexandra, was in a kind of twilight zone between other guests and the servants' quarters. On one side was a room usually allotted to transients—the Alexandra thought of itself as a family residential hotel—and on the other side dwelt Mrs. Pond, the hotel's social director.

It was an inflated title for the somewhat spiritless activities that went on at the Alexandra, or would have been except for Mrs. Pond. Lithe, mid-thirtyish, invariably in black as though it had been invented for her, she had a low husky voice, wise green eyes, and the gift of making an assemblage for bingo seem as exciting as though naughty movies were about to be shown. Somehow she had maneuvered the management into providing her with a small office in the corner of the lobby, furnished with cypress and lime tweed, and here, with the chef, she plotted the intricacies of old Mrs. Blaine's birthday dinner party or, with the manager, discussed the feasibility of a weekly puppet show for the many children who swarmed about the place. She was decorative in the dining room every evening; it was thought that a great many single men, and possibly a few others, came back to the Alexandra because of Mrs. Pond.

She was also surprisingly and genuinely friendly. She and Celia encountered each other often in their corridor, and a smiling, "Good morning, Miss Brett" became "Raining—and I *just* had my hair done," and one evening when they were both waiting for the elevator down there was a small electric sound and a shoulder strap of Mrs. Pond's black taffeta flew free.

Mrs. Pond uttered a simple longshoreman's expletive. Celia recoiled somewhat, because she admired the other woman immensely, but said, "Oh, what a shame. I have a needle and thread in my room, if you like. It wouldn't take a minute."

"But I couldn't possibly ask you—"

"No, I mean it, really."

Mrs. Pond allowed herself to be conducted back to Celia's room and stood still while Celia ministered expertly to the strap. She said as they emerged into the corridor again, "Thank you so much, I couldn't have changed so fast and I'm on the brink of being late. If there's anything I can do to make you more comfortable here, please let me know."

From there it was only a step to an occasional evening chat in one room or the other. Celia could not place the social director—in her limited experience married working women were drudges, and attractive, sleek women were inclined to be haughty—but she sensed that there would be no danger to her even if Mrs. Pond knew her life history; that her reaction, in fact, might be amused admiration.

But she did not take the chance; she was never to do that. She said that she wondered—perhaps Mrs. Pond knew?—what opportunities there might be for a girl in New York apart from secretarial work. She had no specific training, and although she had a little money saved, her resources were slipping away.

"How well I know," murmured Mrs. Pond. She gazed appraisingly at Celia. "Are you English, by the way?"

"No . . ." It must have been lodged in Celia's brain somewhere for perhaps just this moment, because it came out without effort: "I had an English nurse once."

"Hmm," said Mrs. Pond; there was no way of knowing how she had received that. "Have you ever thought of modeling? Clothes? It's not quite the breeze it's cracked up to be, I'm told—still, you're tall and you have a very good figure . . . but I don't know a soul on Seventh Avenue."

She lapsed into brooding thought, from which she roused herself to say, "I'll tell you what I *would* do, right away. Please give me a Christian burial if I'm struck by lightning for saying this, but I'd move out of the hotel and take an apartment with another girl while you're looking around—you'd cut your expenses way down. Of course, you have to watch out for the weird ones, but it's considered quite a smart thing to do."

They were in Celia's room, and Mrs. Pond stood up in her slender black and gave a gingerly stretch. "Time to go and soak what Mr. Hochstedt has left of my toes," she remarked in a parenthetical way, and then, reflectively, "I know the Culhanes' daughter didn't go back to Bennington this year—she's working in the research department of a

61

news magazine and sharing an apartment. Having been over the ground so recently she might be able to suggest something. I can ask, if you like."

But where Celia was going she did not want anyone, however likable, to be able to follow later. She said hastily, "It's certainly something to think about," and did, while the rush of her bath water matched that of the neighboring bath a few minutes later.

Hotels, or at any rate this one, had nothing more to teach her: what had seemed an adventure on her monthly weekend away from Stedman Circle had become a bore. There was undoubtedly money here, but it was the kind of money that prudently decided that the mink would do for another season, and in any case it was not only wealth that Celia admired, it was lustre as well. From conversation garnered in the lobby and dining room, expensive orthodontists for their grandchildren was as lustrous as the guests at the Alexandra were apt to become.

Just as she had once tried to model herself on Mrs. Stevenson in that far-distant time, Celia now took a second mentor in Mrs. Pond. Immediately after breakfast the next morning she carried her newspaper to a nearby park—even in repose she had such an air of purpose that she was quite safe in parks—and began studying the apartments-for-rent section. Her eye quickly learned to single out the words "Will share" from the close-massed type, and when she rose from the bench she had marked five possibilities, all of which said to call after five-thirty P.M.

Celia was well aware that her success so far had sprung largely from her air of calm certainty and her ability to adapt to new requirements. She could not familiarize herself with modeling ahead of time, but she could at least take a preliminary look at Seventh Avenue. She had covered one crosstown and two downtown blocks when a man in an Alpine hat, waiting for a light on the opposite corner, flung up an arm in urgent greeting; his voice was lost in traffic but his lips seemed to be shaping "Wait."

Willis Lambert? Celia was torn between protective freezing and panic flight, and was spared either because she was pushed impatiently aside by a woman who began to wave in return at the Alpine-hatted stranger. But she was badly shaken at her own carelessness in assuming that once she had removed herself from New Jersey she had left that particular area of the past behind her for good. Now, in a number of rapidly superimposed scenes, she saw Willis returning ardently from Milwaukee, finding the "For Sale" sign at 4 Stedman Circle, and learning without much difficulty that the owner, a Mr. Tomlinson, had died in June and left the place to his housekeeper.

Where, Willis would want to know, could he locate the niece who had lived with Mr. Tomlinson?

He must be mistaken. For the last several years Mr. Tomlinson had lived alone, with only a housekeeper in residence . . .

Celia had by now gained enough insight to realize that although under ordinary circumstances Willis would be furious at having been deceived by a domestic employee, the fact of her inheritance would change matters entirely: his brain would make the nimble leap from bold duplicity to innocent mischief. And, by the same token, he would pursue her all the more zealously.

Celia felt thoroughly capable of handling that part of it. But what if he should penetrate the Hotel Alexandra and pass under the knowledgeable green eye of Mrs.

Pond? ("I had an English nurse once.") What if he should turn drunkenly and publicly boastful?

She had left the hotel with her usual free, unhurried stride; she returned to it far more speedily. In her room she called her lawyer, ostensibly to find out whether he had tried to reach her—"I've been out of town for a few days."

"Well, no," said Mr. Agnew, "but I believe we'll have some good news for you by the end of the week. I have a dentist—they're the ones with the ready cash these days, eh?—who wants the house badly. I'm assuming you'd be willing to sacrifice a couple of hundred dollars, if necessary, in favor of an immediate sale?"

Celia said yes, although even in her present anxiety it went against the grain. "Oh, by the way," she added casually but firmly, "I'd rather that you didn't give out my address to anyone just now. I'm so unsettled that I'd prefer to do any getting in touch myself. I don't suppose anyone has asked?"

This necessitated some interoffice inquiries, and then, "Just a Mr. Lambert," said Mr. Agnew.

He assured her that his secretary had taken the call and that no information had been given out, but the Alpine hat had certainly been an omen. Celia applied herself fiercely to her apartment hunting in the conviction that she would be far more invisible as the roommate of a stranger than anywhere else: for one thing, the telephone would be listed under a name other than hers.

But it was not as simple as Mrs. Pond had seemed to think it. The first of Celia's marked possibilities did not answer, the second had already found someone, thank you.

The third inquired distrustfully, "Do you have a stereo?" It was impossible to discern whether the answer wanted were negative or affirmative. Celia said no, truthfully, and the voice said with regret, "That's too bad, because I have all these marvelous albums and nothing to play them on. I guess I'd better put that in the ad."

The fourth number was so garrulous and eager that she sounded like one of Mrs. Pond's weird ones. "*Actually* it's just one great huge room," she confided (the ad had read studio apt.) "but I've done the cunningest things with screens and the possibilities are *endless*. I have a real wood-burning fireplace, that's always so cosy, don't you think, and my cat adores new people, doesn't he?" This addressed to the cat. "I'll be in all evening if you'd care to come by."

The fifth and last advertiser was a crisp and chilly voice belonging to a nurse on a hospital night shift, and the division of duties and meal-preparing and entertaining privileges sounded daunting. Celia tried the first number again without success, went down to dinner, presently retired for the night, and, in the morning, bought two newspapers.

On the fourth day of her search she came upon Mary Ellen Vestry, who had already had one disaster in her life.

Celia had spoken to perhaps thirty strange feminine voices. Because it had a diffident quality lacking in the others, she pounced upon this one at once, much as a miner might pounce upon a demure-looking lump with the conviction that there was something very valuable inside. The preliminaries over, she said firmly that the apartment sounded like just what she had been looking for—it hadn't; the rent was more than she had hoped to pay—and might she come and see it right away?

"Well . . . I'm on my way out now, as a matter of fact," said the voice with an air of hasty improvisation. "Would eight o'clock be convenient? It's Apartment 4A, and I'm Mary Ellen Vestry. Oh, and I'm afraid the elevator isn't working tonight. It seems to be something to do with the rain, although how *that* . . ."

Celia was to become accustomed to these puzzled irrelevancies. Now she only said with renewed briskness that she would be there at eight, and hung up with an excitement that she was presently able to trace to its source. Even this hotel was a link with the past, sheltering her as it had on the weekends when she had watched and listened and learned; it held, however faintly, the ghost of a maid-turned-housekeeper. The Celia Brett who left it for good could become whoever she wished.

Although it was barely six she called room service, a rare extravagance for her, and ordered a sandwich and coffee. She was dressed and ready to leave by seven; she filled the interval determinedly with a magazine, with the result that when she finally picked up her bag and gloves she almost succeeded in surprising herself in the mirror as she might appear to Mary Ellen Vestry.

Tall; fair hair wound smoothly into a chignon, a fugitive glimmer of the Bonwit Teller pearls at the throat of her tailored raincoat: there was no trace of any deferential tray-carrying in that self-possessed carriage. It was true that she looked very faintly foreign—an automatic avoidance of starches and desserts, plus her natural thrift, had placed slight hollows under her broad cheekbones—but it was in an assured rather than a bewildered way.

From the fluster in her young-sounding voice, the Vestry

girl had almost certainly wanted time to call someone in to help pass judgment. Celia was bolstered up by her own reflection. It was still raining, and she tied a scarf loosely at the nape of her neck—anything knotted under the chin stripped away a whole generation of her forebears—and, in her second luxury of the evening, took a taxi to the apartment-house address.

She was impressed at once. She could not actually bring to mind its former tubbed evergreens or doorman or crimson carpeting, but even to her eyes the lobby, now ornamented only with a dim mirror, a table, an urn full of sand and a long strip of black rubber matting, had an air of past opulence. She mounted four flights of stairs, each broken by a half-landing, and was met at the top by a girl in front of an open door marked 4A.

"You're Celia Brett, and I'm sorry about the stairs— that sounds silly, doesn't it? I mean I'm Mary Ellen Vestry, and come on in and catch your breath."

She was as young as Celia had guessed, possibly twenty-two, with a waifish look which was then fashionable but seemed in her case to have sprung from some real illness. Her small face was almost luminescently pale, dark-rimmed glasses so large that they might have come from a disguise kit pointed up her gray eyes, her short light-brown hair clung about her head with the silky helplessness of a child's.

She wore a blue-and-white-striped top and a pair of navy jeans into which a boy of ten could have fitted easily, but the magazine-tutored Celia recognized her sandals as imports. She said over her shoulder, ushering the way up a narrow hall stacked with cartons, "You're seeing the place at its worst, I'm afraid, I'm not really settled yet, but

67

that's just as well because you'd—well, anyone would— have things that you'd want to . . ."

They had reached the doorway of a long, radiant, deep-windowed living room. The girl said with evident relief, "My sister, Susan . . . David MacIntosh."

Introductions were exchanged, along with remarks about what a rainy night it was. Although Susan Vestry, an older and more poised version of her sister, had been sharing a couch with the man, he obviously belonged to Mary Ellen: her face had lit to a glow. Celia did not stare, although a peculiar warmth crept in around the edges of her consciousness. She followed her hostess on a tour of the apartment: small but complete kitchen, tiny pantry, half-bath, full bath, good-sized bedroom across the hall from a slightly smaller one. She hardly heard the trailing commentary: "The landlord says he'll put another towel rack in, but do you suppose he really will?" and "That isn't much of a view unless you're crazy about garbage cans, but the people seem to be quiet."

The man back there in the living room was not Hugh Stevenson, and did not even resemble him, but something —the way his hair grew at the back of his head, or his height or his easy stance—was uncannily reminding. Celia had not consciously resented her banishment after that swift mistaken kiss, and it was with surprise that she listened to an inner voice saying with fierce pleasure, "There is no Mrs. Stevenson here."

"Well, that's it," said Mary Ellen Vestry, leading the way out into the hall again. Her left hand, ringless, although it would not have mattered, had gone out to the wall switch in the second bedroom. "Do you think . . . is

68

this what you had in mind?"

Celia was not given to easy social smiles, but she smiled now, a little downwardly, because Mary Ellen was small. "Very much so," she said.

Eight

Celia had been correct in her assumption that even in the impersonality of New York her background would be inquired into, however politely and indirectly. After her first look at Mary Ellen and the realization that this was the opportunity she had been hoping for, she had decided upon a scrap of conversation overheard at Mr. Tomlinson's house. As well as sounding selfless and noble, it had the virtue of accounting for her lack of friends.

Not that there was anything as crude as an outright question; Susan Vestry, who seemed to be in charge of this aspect, merely led the conversation to the very edge of inviting little silences. Into one of these, Celia remarked that she had only been living in New York for a few weeks: her mother's final illness, at their home in Connecticut, had been a lengthy one.

"The doctor suggested a nursing home, and I suppose there are good ones, but . . ." She gazed pensively down at her hands, which in the last few seconds had more than justified their unmistakable traces of physical labor, and

70

then up again with a forthright air of not wanting to inflict her troubles on others. "Luckily there was a little money left, and New York seemed like the best place to look for a job."

She could not have given a wiser account of herself. There was a sympathetic and admiring glance from Mary Ellen, an impulsive murmur of "I'm sure you won't have any trouble" from Susan Vestry. The man glanced at Celia over a match he was holding to his cigarette, but she sensed approval from that quarter as well.

In return, she learned that the Vestry family lived on Long Island, and that this apartment sprang from Mary Ellen's newly acquired job at a nearby bookshop. She worked for fun, Celia thought with certainty and not a trace of bitterness; this was, after all, exactly the atmosphere at which she had been aiming. In fact, Mary Ellen seemed altogether like one of the girls the fashion magazines were so fond of: the well-bred baby leaving the nest to try her wings in the city, the family solicitude shown with careful casualness in the presence, tonight, of the older sister.

There was certainly money in the background. Even in her relative ignorance of New York wage scales Celia was sure that no bookstore job could support this apartment with its soft gray walls and parquet floors that gleamed between brilliant rugs with odd sharp patterns—Navajo, she found later. Just as certainly, Mary Ellen had been ill not long ago. Discounting the delicate boning of small face and hands, because her taller, darker haired sister shared that, there was a very faint bluey-lavender about her eyes, like a bruise straining to penetrate the silky skin. In the world where Celia had grown up there was a bald answer

71

to this depleted appearance, but it was clearly not the case with the Vestrys of Long Island.

At some point an invisible signal passed, because Mary Ellen jumped out of the chair where she had been curled and said gaily, "It's all settled then. Heavens, what a bad hostess I am. Who'd like coffee, or a drink?"

Intuition told Celia to decline with a smile; Susan Vestry rose too after a glance at her watch. David MacIntosh looked at the rainy windows and said that he could be persuaded to have a drink but would go down with them and find a cab first.

"David, I've been getting cabs in the rain for years," said Susan, and after arrangements that Celia would move in within the next day or two the door of 4A closed behind them and they walked down the stairs. In her single-minded confidence, her mingled respect and contempt for someone cosseted and weak, Celia did not care in the least that Mary Ellen now had David to herself.

Stairs were not the best place for conversation, but Susan Vestry managed it. "What kind of job had you thought of, Celia, if you don't mind my calling you that?"

"I certainly hope you will . . . Someone suggested modeling, although I'm afraid I have no experience with that or anything else, really. What with Mother—"

"Of course," said Susan Vestry quickly. "Let's see . . ." They had arrived in the outer vestibule with its banks of mailboxes. "I know a woman on one of the trade papers, and she just might be able to help, or know someone who could."

"Oh, I don't want to be a nuisance—"

"No nuisance at all," said Susan, "so why don't you let me call around a little before you do anything definite? I think, by the way, that you're going to be very good for Mary Ellen." She opened the outer door and they were under the hollowly echoing canopy, with bright little bounces of rain on the wet sidewalk. "There's usually a cab on University. Can I drop you off?"

"Thank you, but I love to walk," said Celia, knotting her scarf dexterously at her nape. "Maybe it was being cooped up so much . . ."

And she did like to walk—in her exhilaration, had to walk. On this particular night, she could have walked through a blizzard.

Tall for her age, Celia had gone out baby-sitting by the time she was eleven. At fourteen she had been an important economic factor in the taken-in washing and ironing; at sixteen she had become a "mother's helper" in houses which knew the presence of a mother sporadically if at all. Her initial adjustment to the sharing of an apartment was more difficult than any of these undertakings.

She had never lived on equal terms with a contemporary like this one; that was a strain in itself. For all of her adult life her late evenings had been her own after whatever hard day's work: not even demanding Mrs. Stryker would have dared to summon her after a certain point. Mary Ellen Vestry chattered companionably, and borrowed or offered face cream or nail polish or earrings at any hour. She penetrated Celia's existence as relentlessly as a child confident that it is liked.

Moreover, she had habits that set Celia's teeth on edge for the first few days. She was untidy; she had no concept of time; even with her glasses on she had a knack for overturning containers and dropping things. When something urgent occurred to her, she thought nothing of issuing out of her shower with a half-draped towel or nothing at all. Celia, untroubled by any vision of straining old fingers at a balcony's edge, was genuinely scandalized by this.

But on the whole she had a sense of enormous achievement, so much so that she was hardly surprised at the ease with which she was accepted into Mary Ellen's world. On that first evening she had offered to get some of her own furniture out of storage "although it's a little heavy for an apartment, I'm afraid"—if it became necessary she would subtract a few items from Stedman Circle—and when this suggestion was turned down, predictably, she said, "Well, then, just a few sentimental things," and departed to a secondhand store on Third Avenue. Here she bought a faintly spotted old mirror with gilt rosebuds, a small hand-painted china box which looked to her like something an invalid old lady could not have done without, and a fat brown earthenware teapot: with all her Georgian silver, Mrs. Stevenson had treasured one very much like it.

Thus established, Celia settled down to a quiet and thorough appraisal of her new situation. David MacIntosh was never far from her thoughts, although he worked in Providence and only appeared at the apartment on weekends, and she speculated a good deal on what had given Mary Ellen her peculiarly vulnerable look. Neither preoccupation showed; if anything, she evinced less than the normal amount of interest in her roommate's life and the man with whom the roommate was so clearly in love.

Mrs. Cannon and Mr. Tomlinson could have warned Mary Ellen about this appearance of serene self-containment, but Mrs. Cannon was unaware of Mary Ellen's existence and the grass had long been green on Mr. Tomlinson's grave.

Susan Vestry seldom said things she didn't mean, and on a dark afternoon in late November Celia sat in the small cluttered office of Charlotte Wise, who was presently studying her as inquisitively as a Pekingese.

Mrs. Wise was associate editor of a trade paper which was infinitely less glamorous than the magazines Celia pored over and wielded infinitely more power in the fashion world. A tiny, swarthy, tirelessly busy woman, she had seen Celia at all only because she liked Susan Vestry, and was prolonging the interview beyond a rapidly scribbled memo because the girl puzzled her.

It wasn't a matter of physical characteristics, although there was something intriguing about the set of the dark eyes and the faintly foreign upper half of the face, combined with the occasional touch of English accent. Nor was it the vastly becoming leopard coat, which Mrs. Wise's expert eye identified as four years old: like most other editors in the field of fashion journalism she had her share of aging debutantes bored with lunches at the Colony and eager to try the treadmill.

It was her manner, which "self-possessed" didn't begin to describe. From the outset, the older woman had the half-amused, half-annoyed feeling that it was she who was being studied and evaluated. Celia Brett emanated an aura of fathomless experience, although she couldn't have been past her mid-twenties and reportedly had never worked before; there was something about nursing an invalid mother.

The thought rippled through Charlotte Wise's mind that

75

she wouldn't have cared to change places with the mother. On the other hand—she reached for a memo pad and began to scrawl decisively on it—the kind of job in question did not require any compassion, and the girl undeniably had something. She extended the note, was thanked composedly, and, when she was alone again, picked up her receiver and dialed.

". . . Harry? Charlotte Wise. I've sent over a girl, a tall 14, who ought to look absolutely marvelous in your stuff. Her name is Brett and she's wearing a leopard coat which I'm not a *hundred* per cent sure comes off. Even if you haven't anything for her right now I'd keep her on file . . ."

The Seventh Avenue manufacturer who was Castletweed had been called out of his office by the time she found her way there, which would mean going back on Monday morning, but Celia was undismayed. She was well aware that the leopard coat might have been made for her instead of bought that morning at a charity thrift shop; in it, with her free and effortless walk, she drew more than an occasional following glance. In it she looked like someone who, if she worked at all, did it for fun.

The sale of 4 Stedman Circle had gone through three days earlier. Even after the commission and lawyer's fee and other expenses, the remaining sum would once have seemed to Celia enough for a lifetime. She knew better now, but she also knew that, for her, a few really good clothes would be a better investment than the best of blue-chip stocks.

And certain economies, she had discovered, were not only permissible but actually smart; she had encountered some astonishing women at the thrift shop. She had gone there in the assumption since adolescence that mink was the ultimate in furs, but in the only mink jacket available she had looked like no one more unusual than a highly paid secretary.

But the leopard, shading from almost the color of Celia's hair to smoked gold among the thickening black, seemed less a new identity than the completion of one. It was slightly worn around the turned-back cuffs and the high collarless throat, but she could have the cuffs cut off, possibly, and a round collar made. She would say casually, when Mary Ellen asked, that she had just taken it out of storage.

. . . Mary Ellen was home already, a good hour ahead of time. The apartment was silent, but there were lamps on in the living room and the familiar big black calfskin bag, a jacketed novel poking out of it, was tossed with her gloves on a chair. The small kitchen was dark, but so, apparently, was Mary Ellen's room. Celia stood in the hall outside it for a considering moment and then tapped. A shift of weight on the bed and a faint murmur answered her.

"Mary Ellen? Are you all right?"

"Hi . . . come on in, but don't turn on the light," said Mary Ellen muffledly from within, and Celia opened the door with a caution in no way betrayed by her great and sudden leap of curiosity.

The bedroom faced the street, and reflected light from the ceiling and the windows of the apartment house opposite showed her Mary Ellen lying motionless on her back, a cloth over her eyes. "Headache," she said in the drowned-sounding voice, obviously keeping the effort of speech to a minimum.

"I've got something awfully good for that," said Celia, and was stopped in mid-turn by a fast, flat "No, thanks. It'll go away."

"But it's only—"

"Please, *no*," interrupted Mary Ellen with the nearest approach to anger Celia had heard from her. There was an electric little silence, announcing that this reaction came from something more than pain. Perhaps in an attempt to decharge it, Mary Ellen said, "Would you get me a fresh cloth, though?"

In the bathroom, under the covering sound of running water, Celia opened the medicine cabinet—she herself had taken over the half-bath—and gave it a thoughtful inspection. The only concession to pain or sleeplessness or nerves was a stark little bottle of aspirin, which was odd, surely, in a girl of Mary Ellen's fragile appearance? She wrung out the cloth, brought it in and offered tea in a carefully neutral tone. "Or would you rather just be left alone?"

"No, I'd like a cup of tea. You've probably gathered that I'm—funny about drugs." Had she heard the cautious click of the cabinet door? The dimness hid a defensive flush but it was certainly there, just as there was a decision balanced between the long drawing-in and expelling of a breath. "The fact is that I had a—a very bad time a year ago."

The circumstances called upon Celia to murmur, "Don't tell me if you'd rather not," or "Don't talk if it hurts your head." Instead, she said encouragingly, "Oh, did you?"

"I was in a car crash that killed three people. One of them was the man I was going to marry. He was just back from Vietnam and we were driving to the country club because some people were giving a party for us. To cele-brate." Mary Ellen spoke in a kind of halting rush, as though this had to be said rapidly or not at all. "The other car came straight at us, on the wrong side of a divided highway."

Perhaps because of the words, and a lull in traffic, the slamming of a car door in the street below had a surpris-ingly personal and imminent sound. David MacIntosh, down from Providence for the weekend? wondered Celia with an edge of her tight attention—although she had al-ready guessed what was coming next.

It was still startling to hear it said in the painfully chosen phrases. Mary Ellen, sole and nearly miraculous survivor of the crash, had had a nervous breakdown after her release from the hospital, contributed to by the with-drawal of the morphine on which she had become depen-dent. Ex-drug addict, thought Celia, applying the term coolly and experimentally to the image of the short silky hair, the big gray eyes, the imported sandals.

A faint shuddering vibration announced that the ele-vator had reached the fourth floor, and Mary Ellen caught her breath like someone reprieved. "If that's David, I'm not fit to be seen. I think he has theater tickets, so would you go with him, Celia? I honestly wish you would. Sleep's the only thing that's going to do me much good."

In the end, she prevailed. Celia prepared her tea and toast, and went to get dressed with an exultation un-clouded by the strange little flicker of David's eyes when he learned of the changed plans. By the law of averages it had had to happen sooner or later—even protected Mary Ellen wasn't proof against occasional indisposition—but tonight it seemed like a gift laid astonishingly in her lap.

She had never been to the theater, and she was going tonight. In her leopard coat, with Mary Ellen's man. There was no one to say, "Don't touch"—and she was sure that, more than once, she had felt his speculative gaze on her although it slipped immediately away.

It did not slip away this evening. Drinks ordered, David MacIntosh looked at her across the restaurant table, a steady, measuring, hazel look, and said pleasantly, "At the risk of sounding rude, hadn't we both better know where we stand? You put up a very good front—in fact, Mary Ellen still hasn't a suspicion—but I've known, almost from the beginning."

Nine

The blood stood incredulously still in Celia's body. It wasn't possible that the yellow snap of Mrs. Cannon's eyes could see this far, could hunt her out and destroy her without warning, and yet—

Total shock and disbelief rendered her incapable of answering at all. She simply stared at the man opposite, and her very speechlessness was her salvation. "I might have known Mrs. Vestry wouldn't give in so easily," he went on stubbornly but far less certainly. "The whole point of— You *are* in that apartment, aren't you, to keep an eye on Mary Ellen?"

Celia thought later that it would have been politic to register outrage that she could have been suspected of any deception at all. At the moment, her feeling of relief was so enormous, like discovering a precipice edge to be only a single grassy step down, that she simply said, "I had never heard of Mary Ellen until I answered her ad, and I've never met her mother or anyone else in the family but her sister."

The drinks came. Celia continued to meet the hazel gaze, her heart still beating heavily with reaction, and watched it change from distrust to an almost ludicrous embarrassment. The thin face—"nice" seemed as accurate a description as any—relaxed. David said, "I beg your pardon. The circumstances looked so very—"

He broke off, obviously aware that this could be a troublesome tack, and changed direction. "Mrs. Vestry is one of those wildly overprotective mothers. Mary Ellen's her youngest—there's a married son who took his practice out to the West Coast—and she's always been cast as the baby. Maybe that's natural enough up to a point but it can be pretty oppressive too, and after Mary Ellen was badly injured in a car crash Mrs. Vestry got absolutely obsessive. Everybody agreed that Mary Ellen had to get out of her mother's shadow, and Mrs. Vestry finally gave in about the New York apartment on condition that she share it. And you turned up on the dot, so obviously steady and upright and even with some experience in . . ."

Someone else's face might have flamed at this description. Celia regarded her companion tranquilly. "In nursing. Mary Ellen told me about her—illness," she said as easily as though the knowledge were not quite two hours old and then imparted under stress. "I still don't know what made you think anyone at all was spying."

And she didn't know, although the uneasy speculation had crossed her mind that, because of his special relationship with Mary Ellen, this man had somehow plucked her own concentration out of the air and placed an entirely wrong interpretation on it.

"Well, Mary Ellen and I have been out there to dinner twice in the last three weeks, and Mrs. Vestry seems extremely well-informed."

"Then it must be someone who goes to the bookstore and pumps Mary Ellen," said Celia firmly and, as it turned out, accurately. "She's very"— she had to hunt for a word that would not make him bristle—"unsuspecting."

"She is, isn't she?" agreed David eagerly, and noticed his drink and lifted it to her, smiling; not a smile connected with Mary Ellen this time, but just for Celia. "No grudge?"

Celia would have liked to respond with something light and witty, but, although she did not recognize it, and in time would acquire standard responses to standard situations, real lightness was as alien to her as a bone to a banana. So she returned his smile and only said, "Of course not." David MacIntosh could not have guessed at how sincerely she meant it.

His accusation, and subsequent embarrassment and need for explanation, had established a peculiar intimacy between them that could never have come simply from their both, theoretically, being devoted to Mary Ellen. They were a little like adults discussing a marvelous child. It might have been considered a dubious bond, but for the moment Celia was content with it.

The theater seats were good ones, but after her first genuine shock of surprise at the close actuality of flesh-and-blood players and the odd resonance of voices and footsteps on the stage, she barely followed the play itself. The central character seemed to be a waspish man in a dressing gown, while other people came and went through an astonishing number of doors and windows—at amusing intervals, apparently, because little tides of laughter rippled through the theater. Celia heard it all from a distance; she was overridingly conscious of David's profile beside her, his hand under her elbow as they navigated up the aisle at intermission.

At no point was it love, or even strong physical attraction. It was triumph, the headier because it was secret. It was all the Mrs. Stevensons in the world, with all their desirable and out-of-bounds sons, powerless now to dismiss Celia from the scene.

In the lobby, just before the third-act buzzer, David turned in response to a tap on his shoulder, said with obvious pleasure, "Spence . . . Helen. When did you get back?" and seconds later was introducing Celia to a darkly tanned, amazingly bald man and a pretty woman with polished black bangs and a beautiful figure. They had evidently just returned from Majorca.

After a desultory comment or two about the play ("Clifton Webb really did it for all time, but Langley is very good") tentative arrangements were made to meet for a drink afterwards—and in the middle of them something made a small, computerlike click in Celia's head. Turning a little aside, audible only to David, she murmured, "I'd love to, but I think I really ought to get back, you know."

And for just a second, David looked blank before he said, "Oh. You're right, of course."

For another second, Mary Ellen hung in the air, a very slight nuisance with her headache. That was some reward, but Celia, for tactical reasons deprived of a visit to a fabled after-theater place and the company of this dazzlingly knowledgeable-looking couple, was determined not to let it rest at that. At the curb, in the midst of the struggle over cabs, she said with an air of impulsiveness, "Let's walk a little way, shall we?"

David looked at her with pleased surprise, as well he

might; Mary Ellen made wry little sagas of her walks with him. ("Only a few blocks, he said, but that must have been before they moved Central Park.") He could hardly fail to notice the freedom with which Celia moved, or the more companionable height of her shoulders. When a taxi did slow, and they took it as a matter of course, there was a faint unspoken suggestion of regret, as though someone had come along with an umbrella just when they were enjoying the rain.

Small, dimly lit elevators were intimate at that hour. Celia said, "Thank you very much, David. I shouldn't have enjoyed myself so much, with poor Mary Ellen ill, but I'm afraid I did."

"So did I," said David. "You're quite a walker," and waited until Celia turned her key. "Better not come in, we don't want to wake her," she whispered over her shoulder, and although David had had no intention of going in, there was, again, the wraith of the untasted nightcap, the leisurely rehash of the play. Celia summoned a kind of decorous complicity with her soft "Good night" and gentle closing of the door.

Mary Ellen was very much awake, sitting up and reading. Out of some subconscious defensiveness she had brushed her hair and put on a tangerine bed-jacket that threw a faint glow up into her small face. A trace of her cool sharp cologne lingered on the air. Celia, who had found it politic to hurry home to the sufferer, knew an instant of pure, uncomplicated dislike. "Is your head better?"

"Much, thanks. Practically like new. How was the play?"

"Marvelous, although I felt guilty about taking over

your seat like that." Rapidly, before the other girl could begin to ask for details which she couldn't supply, Celia said, "Anything I can do for you before I go to bed? It's been a long day, what with tramping around on interviews."

"Not a thing. *What* a stunning coat, is it new?"

It wasn't mockery—Mary Ellen was probably myopic enough to believe that the coat was new—but somehow the friendly talkativeness was tearing the evening's triumph to pieces. She said with a slight edge, "No, I just got it out of storage," and yawned and stretched with exaggeration. In the doorway she said punishingly, "Funny, the way you can be physically tired and all wound up at the same time. I haven't your scruples, so I think I'll take a sleeping pill . . ."

Celia was asked to the Vestrys' for Christmas weekend, partly, she suspected, because Mary Ellen didn't know quite what else to do about her, and partly because she would help serve as a buffer against the formidable Mrs. Vestry.

In the meantime, Harry Bloom had taken shrewd stock of Celia and she had done a little modeling for Castletweed. It was not, she discovered, the kind of modeling associated with chic hatboxes and extravagant eye make-up and other glamorous trappings; it was a matter of parading new Castletweed designs on echoing bare boards before little groups of hard-eyed buyers, often while someone darted agilely behind her and seized the fabric at waist or hips. But Celia herself sometimes caused a faint tired interest, perhaps because the people of this particular world saw so many conventional moist-lipped beauties, and an eager young hireling took her picture in a buckled cape, with an electric fan to set her long pale hair streaming, which subsequently appeared in a trade journal.

She had not been out alone with David again, although Mary Ellen arranged occasional foursomes, but the relationship between them had undergone a change. On evenings when he waited with a drink for Mary Ellen to find a scarf or a belt or even, on one occasion, a pair of shoes, Celia was no longer a lay figure—the roommate—but feminine in her own right, the companion of an exhilarating night walk. She sensed that it would be disastrous to pit her own calm and certitude of movement against Mary Ellen's charming ineptitude, because while ants might do the work grasshoppers were much more popular, but more than once she and David smiled at each other in an *alone* way across the room.

On the fifteenth of December, Mary Ellen said at breakfast, "If you haven't any other plans for Christmas, Celia, why not come home with me?"

"Oh, I don't think I should, do you? It's such a family time," said Celia with an air of wistful recollection. No observer would have guessed that for the past several years she had managed to confine her own sentimental feelings in this regard to a Christmas card and a ten-dollar bill.

"You'd only stay here and brood, which nobody should do at Christmas," said Mary Ellen firmly. "Besides which, you'll be more than welcome. Mother's been wanting to meet you. I'll have her call you if that will make you feel any better about it."

It would be the first time in her life that Celia had slept in anyone's home as a guest. Instead of redoubling her labors in an employer's house as Christmas approached, *she* would be the one to arrive, the object and not the supplier of the fresh linen and towels and attention. For the briefest of instants, in some strange, transported way, she gazed with wonder at the simple fact of this achievement.

But even after Mrs. Vestry called the next day, in a voice resembling gravel being poured down a chute, Celia was in doubt as to what to bring or, if necessary, buy. Mary Ellen, clearly assuming that she had been a house guest on other occasions and had certainly attended Christmas parties, was no help; she only said blithely, "Oh, good, that's settled," and returned to her gift-wrapping. This was a process which the deft Celia could hardly bear to watch: under Mary Ellen's tutelage, festive paper flew apart, ribbon slipped from corners, the scissors got lost. Irritatingly, she seemed to enjoy the shambles, and looked on with an air of slight regret when Celia, driven beyond endurance, whisked paper and ribbon into taut perfection without wasting an inch of anything. "I suppose it's something like perfect pitch," observed Mary Ellen unenviously. "You either have it or you don't."

In the end, Celia had to ask carelessly, "Will I be needing an evening dress?"

"Better bring one," said Mary Ellen vaguely, as though Celia had several instead of none at all. "You never know, we might get roped into something at the country club. Oh, I go there. David made me see that I had to."

David, who would be on the scene at some point over Christmas although he had his own family obligations. . . . Celia bought an evening dress of pale-blonde brocade, completely simple except for a narrow ribbon of icy yellow satin at the midriff; in it, she looked as serene as a

88

candle. But her real weapon was a pair of shoes for walking.

Mary Ellen had somehow wangled her way out of the frantically busy bookshop by five o'clock on Christmas Eve. Celia, wearing the leopard coat and the one good suit she had promised herself, met her at five thirty at Pennsylvania Station. And there—emerging from the hectic mass of luggage-laden, parcel-carrying, holiday-flushed humanity with the unlikelihood of a needle leaping out of a haystack, she also met Willis Lambert.

Ten

For a moment or two, in spite of the shouted "Celia! Hey, *Celia!*" it almost seemed possible to avoid him. Celia turned her head away and wove rapidly and ruthlessly through the crowd as though she hadn't heard. When Mary Ellen, struggling to keep up with her, panted breathlessly, "Someone's calling you," she answered as though that had been swallowed up in the loud-speaker carols, "Gate seven—we'd better hurry."

But a very small lost child had sat down to cry, and in one of the strange spontaneous departures which overtake New Yorkers at festive seasons, strangers who would normally have scorned to notice each other had stopped to exchange clucks of concern. Helpless with rage at the scented furs of two elderly women who stood immovably in her path, Celia was trapped for the few seconds it took Willis Lambert to navigate the ring from the far side.

And there he stood, breathing hard and reproachfully, disaster made visible in a bright tweed topcoat that fitted too tightly. Even from a distance he had worn an expression of astonishment; now, after the merest flick of a glance at Mary Ellen, he amplified this to an elaborately admiring head-to-toe inspection of Celia and a "Sa-a-ay," that had the quality of a whistle. The leopard coat stirred him to a witticism that was only half-friendly. "Certainly have changed your spots, haven't you, Celia?"

"Oh, hello, Willis—and good-bye for now, I'm afraid, we have a train to catch," said Celia, trying to speak lightly out of a throat that felt turned to stone. "Merry Christmas."

She started to move away as she spoke, and Willis's hand shot out for her gloved wrist. "Oh, no, you don't, not when I've just found you again." He wasn't drunk, but there was a breath of liquor mingling strongly with his hair cream or whatever it was, and his playfulness had a definite bite. In the more than six months since she had seen him he had gained weight; in the midst of her hatred Celia noted that his profile was now plushy rather than wavy, and little pads of fat under the skin were beginning to push upward against his eyes.

Mary Ellen, beside her, was a pinpoint of silent bafflement in the great teeming station; the very lack of introductions bewildered her. Celia glanced at her, said casually between her teeth, "See if you can save me a seat, will you, and I'll meet you on the train," and turned back to Willis. "Are you still working for Temple Insurance?"

Willis nodded proudly. "I get my own territory on the first of the year—how about that? But you're the one I have to hand it to. That was some act you pulled about being the old man's—"

"*Let go of me,*" said Celia with such cold ferocity that his fingers fell away from her wrist at once, "and please don't bother me again."

Speed of comprehension had never been Willis's strongest asset, and now he gaped confusedly for seconds before his face began to fill darkly with color. "Oh? Pretty quick with the brush-off, aren't you? Found yourself another rich *uncle?*"

Celia's fingers clenched around the handle of the suitcase she picked up. "I don't know what you misunderstood," she said, speaking slowly and steadily, "but if you start circulating rumors about me I'll find out, and I'll see that Temple Insurance gets the letters you wrote me from Milwaukee, the ones explaining how much you were making on your expense account. I don't think they'd like that, Willis. I think they might not give you a territory after all. I think you'd find it hard to get a job in any insurance company around here."

She knew instinctively that to wait even momentarily for his reaction would be to diminish the impact of the threat. She walked instantly away at a controlled speed which suggested purpose but not flight, even though from the retained image of murderous rage on Willis's face she half-expected a violent hand on her shoulder. When it did not come, the beginnings of confidence began to warm away a little of her body's fierce tension.

She had no real way of assessing the strength of her weapon, but it stood to reason that strict honesty would be a fairly basic requirement in a claims investigator. It seemed equally plausible that even rival insurance companies would close ranks on such an issue. Besides, she had had no choice. A smile and a false address would have left Willis Lambert lingering underfoot like a land mine on any street corner or in any restaurant, far more dangerous than before. His face had flashed into a distillation of fury disturbing to remember, but surely a man ambitious enough to attend night school wouldn't jeopardize his job to avenge a private humiliation? He had indeed mentioned padding his expense account in Milwaukee, but from a distance of all those months he might easily think the carefully preserved letters far more damaging than they actually were.

An explanation had to be found for Mary Ellen, who had miraculously saved a seat on the crowded train and made herself very unpopular by doing so. Celia transferred the protective heap of handbag and newspaper and packages, sank down, and said with an exasperated air, "Just because I went to a high-school dance with that creature once, he keeps bobbing up and pretending we're old friends. I didn't even dare introduce you for fear he'd start coming around to the apartment."

"He certainly looked the persistent type, but at least you got rid of him," said Mary Ellen cheerfully as the train started, and Celia, with an inner and recoiling wonder that Willis had ever seemed like a trophy to be won, replied, "Yes. For good, I think."

But the encounter, or Willis's jeer, had shaken her in an area where she had begun to feel secure, and in the moment of being introduced to the Vestrys' housekeeper Celia had a brief terror that the older woman would show her a gleam of mocking recognition. "Don't be put off by Mrs. Trask," Mary Ellen had advised in the taxi. "She's been with us since I was five and she never lets me forget it. She looks like a tartar but she really has a heart of gold. At least," she added in one of her characteristic wanderings, "we've always assumed that she has a heart of gold; I don't know whether it's ever been put to the test. It would be ghastly, sort of, if she didn't at all."

But to the housekeeper, for all her shrewd little brown eyes, Celia was merely another guest. She began to fuss over Mary Ellen, and pure reaction gave Celia such a heightened awareness that she never quite forgot that instant in the paneled hall. A sharp fragrance from evergreens piled in a huge copper bowl, a murmur of voices from a room of which only a radiant corner was visible, showing the arm of a flowery slipcovered couch, shining dark curlicues at the edge of a mirror, reflected points of color from an unseen Christmas tree glowing on a pale wall: it was like an essence bottled especially for Celia Brett.

Only one other moment of the weekend was to attain that curious, threshold excitement.

The gravelly voice which Celia had attributed to a bad telephone connection was Mrs. Vestry's very own. Even when she lowered it confidentially it had a deep and roughened quality, like the purr of a cat with a bad cold. She was a tall, angular woman with short, curly, biscuit-colored hair and bright blue eyes, and it never came as a surprise to people meeting her for the first time that she could still beat her husband, her son, and her two daughters at tennis.

It was from their father that both girls inherited their gray eyes and Mary Ellen her look of extreme youth: in spite of his silvering hair, a lock of which usually fell over his forehead, and glasses with a down-trailing black ribbon, Paul Vestry had somewhat the air of a plaintive boy. He was retired—from what, nobody ever said—and had

94

acquired a number of defensive hobbies at which he pottered fiercely.

To Celia it seemed almost possible that people like the Vestrys could summon snow for Christmas Eve: by the time Susan arrived at eleven the ground was covered with a sparkly fall. Celia herself, giving a small casual smile to the maid who assisted at the buffet dinner, had begun to feel at ease in an atmosphere she had hitherto only glimpsed in glossy magazines. Common sense told her that the house could not always wear this festive face, but there was still an unsurprised air about it. To anyone who had lived in the gloom induced by Mrs. Stryker's anxious drawing of draperies against the sun, the mere fact that a snow-dampened Labrador and a dachsund were allowed to fling themselves down on the beautiful rugs said a great deal.

At the same time, Celia had a cool appreciation of what had driven Mary Ellen to flight. Mrs. Vestry's intense preoccupation with the well-being of her younger daughter had a curiously sapping effect: after less than four hours of that penetrating gaze and almost constant catechism—"It seems to me you've lost weight. Are they working you to death in that bookshop?"—Mary Ellen was somehow diminished and her small face was growing fretful. It lit again when Susan answered the telephone and came back to say, "Long distance, for you."

Mary Ellen departed with speed. Celia thought, David. Mrs. Vestry said aggrievedly, "I can't think why that child won't wear contact lenses. She'd be so much more attractive."

"They're her eyes," observed Susan to the Christmas tree. The patience of her tone suggested that she had said

95

this often before, and Mrs. Vestry turned to Celia as a possible ally. "Don't you agree with me? Mary Ellen has really beautiful eyes."

Better to side with the daughters in this, even though Celia had been amazed that anyone with the means to do otherwise would wear those ridiculous frames. She said, temporizing, "Well, in a way, the glasses call attention to her eyes, don't you think?"

Mrs. Vestry would have none of this. "Nonsense. Helen Gilmore wears contact lenses, and *she's* stunning. I believe you met the Gilmores one evening at the theater with David. *The Nettle's Touch*, wasn't it? Anyway, the Gilmores remembered you."

It was said with nothing more than carelessness, because it was obviously clear to Mrs. Vestry that no one would dare set a foot on Mary Ellen's preserve, but Susan's head had turned a little, curiously, and even Paul Vestry's absorption in a velvet-cased set of silver coins seemed suspended. The room which Celia had allowed to grow dreamy around her shot into a sharp and dangerous focus; she had to fight down one of her rare eruptions of rage.

"Oh, were those the Gilmores? I remember a nice-looking couple, the night Mary Ellen had a bad headache and I sat in for her"—the necessity of explaining herself was like gall in her mouth—"but I was really much too excited about the play to catch their names. What with Mother's illness and everything, it was such ages since I'd been to the theater."

Mrs. Vestry had been all unwitting; Susan's gaze had sped across the room like an arrow. But if Susan thought she could be another Mrs. Stevenson, she could think again.

96

Celia spent Christmas morning in a quiet, concentrated absorption of a background which she would one day appropriate, with a few necessary emendations, as her own. Very little escaped her. She kept an almost photographic memory of refracted sunlight catching tiny tongued reflections in the Christmas-tree bulbs, the leisurely breakfast of scrambled eggs and sausages and English muffins, the milk punch that arrived at eleven thirty, the ceremonial bones for the dogs, sensibly not gift-wrapped.

Celia had already exchanged presents with Mary Ellen at the apartment, but was not taken aback at a pair of short white pigskin gloves from Susan; she had prepared for such an emergency. "Now where did I—?" she began, looking about her with an air of perplexity, and went up to her room, returning with a small box for Susan and a glimmering object which she placed reverentially in Mrs. Vestry's startled hands. "It was our Christmas candle, and I'd be so pleased if you'd have it, Mrs. Vestry, and give it a happy home."

The clerk in the secondhand store where Celia supplied herself with instant ancestors had used the last phrase with a cynicism which missed her completely. The candlestick, of carved silver-gilt wood, did have a surprisingly nostalgic appearance; out of either carelessness or cunning, traces of colored wax had been allowed to remain in the trailing garments of trumpet-blowing angels, suggesting a festive overflow. It had cost Celia three dollars.

Mrs. Vestry was looking as touched and embarrassed as her craggy features would permit. "It's charming, Celia, but I couldn't let you—"

"You'd be doing me a great favor, really you would. Storage," said Celia firmly, as though determined to re-

97

store lightness to a sorrowful occasion, "is no place for a Christmas candle."

Mrs. Vestry was finally persuaded to accept, and the ornament was given a place of honor on the mantelpiece. During the small fluster caused by all this, Celia, well-pleased with herself, moved modestly off to a window and stood gazing out at a curve of snowy lawn, white-freighted rhododendrons, a row of low thorny-looking bushes with red berries lining one side of the drive. The sun had gone, and under a gray sky the scene had an almost traditional Christmas-card flavor . . . and Celia was suddenly as cold as though an actual door had yawned open behind her.

The card to her parents, containing ten dollars: had she mailed that herself? She had always been extremely careful in the monthly dispatching of those envelopes; her dread of any possible link to the Bridgeport tenement was such that not even in her anonymity at the Hotel Alexandra had she left them at the desk. But this last one, with the card picked indifferently from a drugstore rack . . .

Her mind's eye followed it as far as the small table just inside the living room doorway where she and Mary Ellen were in the habit of leaving mail, but followed it no farther, no matter how she tried. She hadn't had a stamp, she remembered that much, and she had been distracted by the necessity of having to go out and buy the evening dress which she wasn't apparently going to need after all. Celia's last vision had the envelope lying face up, with her own clear writing taking on the aspect of a billboard.

Nearsighted, heedless Mary Ellen had no doubt stamped it and mailed it with cards of her own, and it was hardly likely that she would have telescoped all those syllables

98

to "Brett." Why should she? She could become interminably interested in things like heavy water or sand-casting, but she was singularly incurious about people's backgrounds.

But—the nonexistent breeze blew more coldly on Celia's back while behind her there were murmurs of "Isn't it lovely?" and "Very Renaissance-looking"—Mary Ellen was also extraordinarily absent-minded. She was quite capable of tucking the envelope into the depths of her huge bag, intending to mail it, and then forgetting all about it.

Perhaps because the encounter with Willis Lambert had been so unsettling, Celia said to Mary Ellen at the first opportunity, "By the way, did you ever mail a card I left on the table with no stamp? I know I didn't, but it disappeared."

"Then I must have," said Mary Ellen reasonably. "I remember that I was going to get stamps at lunch on Monday and all they had were those hideous ones that don't look like real stamps at all—I wonder that they ever get through the mail. I *suppose* they do." Under some quality in Celia's stare she went on hastily, "And yes, now that I think of it, I did pick up yours. I had a few last-minute ones of my own to send, at the shop, and when Susan stopped in on Monday afternoon I gave them all to her to mail."

Celia needed the evening dress after all, for what was apparently a traditional day-after-Christmas party at the country club. Along with the simple glowing brocade she wore an air of tranquil accomplishment that had nothing to do with triumph at entering precincts like these for the

99

first time. She scarcely saw the good-looking face of the escort provided for her by Susan's Navy lieutenant, and it did not disturb her, it filled her with elation, that David MacIntosh's glance fled away from hers.

Although he had arrived at the Inn the day before, and been at the house for cocktails and dinner, she had not had a moment alone with him until this afternoon. A kind of post-holiday somnolence had descended, with the Christmas tree shimmering coldly in its fall of silver and looking as remote as the two sleeping dogs. Celia, alone with David and Mary Ellen in the living room, had risen suddenly, strolled to a window, said into the quilted silence, "You know what I'd love? A walk."

She did not glance at David, lazy in a chair with his arms crossed behind his head, although every ounce of her will was concentrated on him. She said to Mary Ellen, briskly, "Where's a good place to go?"

"Right back to your chair," said Mary Ellen with a horrified face. "Celia, it's *cold* out there."

"I know. That's the idea—a little fast exercise to get rid of those marvelous turkey sandwiches. Oh, well," said Celia carelessly as she started for the hall, "I'm sure I can't get lost."

It was a gamble, but a successful one. Behind her she heard David say, "Come on, my love, just to the Point and back," and Mary Ellen grumble, "Well, all right, but I don't know how I ever got tangled up with such energetic people."

Celia had been resigned to her coming along; for all her random ways Mary Ellen was the kind of hostess who would consider it only courteous to jump over a cliff with her guest if that was what the guest wanted to do. What she hadn't hoped for was that the telephone would ring just as they all neared the door, and Mary Ellen would answer it and say, "Hi, Marge . . . Yes, thanks, did you?" She grimaced at them over the mouthpiece, went on listening, presently flipped her fingers at them in a go-on-ahead gesture.

The world was full of people who said after events, "If I'd only had a chance—" Celia was not among them. She glanced inquiringly at David and opened the door.

She genuinely enjoyed walking—fast, vigorous walking as opposed to strolling—and she knew that it was an activity that became her, as it did not a majority of women, who had to take frequent little running, catching-up steps. As the big houses began to thin, and they turned into a narrow sandy road where the wind was unmistakably right off the water, she became aware of something else: David was as fully conscious as she that they had left Mary Ellen in the house behind them. He kept his arm elaborately from touching hers as they walked, and his silence had the constraint which follows a quarrel between two people closely involved, when the first word spoken may prove of crucial importance.

The peculiar excitement of that waiting moment in the Vestrys' hall came sharply back to Celia, although this time it was compounded of wind and gray water and the crying of gulls as she and David emerged on a small rocky headland. They would either turn around now and go back, or—

"Watch these rocks, they're slippery. Oh, God," said David in an odd abrupt voice, and put out a steadying arm, turned her around and kissed her.

Celia closed her eyes, not from rapture but in order to

101

taste her victory more fully. How many weeks since she had first seen him in the apartment living room, bearing that elusive trace of Hugh Stevenson, all the more attractive because he was a symbol of what she had once been forbidden to touch? How many times had she thought, I *know* he notices me, and pretends he doesn't, and finds me attractive?

His arms dropped. He said in a shaken voice, "We'd better go back," and Celia replied composedly, "Yes, we'd better. In fact"—she had turned, and her faint breathlessness was due neither to his kiss nor the wind—"there's Mary Ellen."

Mary Ellen, a small figure in the distance, was not wearing her glasses, and it was impossible to tell from her manner whether she had seen two blurred shapes merge into one. Or perhaps that was the way people like the Vestrys did things, thought Celia, contemptuous but still a little uneasy; she was somewhat afraid of Mrs. Vestry, in spite of the easy deception with the Christmas candle, and did not want any confrontation here.

There wasn't one. If Mary Ellen was gayer and more talkative than usual at the country club that evening, it was attributable to the holiday season. No one could have said with certainty that she was like someone desperately fanning a spark which threatened to die, or even that she noticed the mutual avoidance of glances that linked Celia and David like a bridge. Susan's clear-eyed assessment was a threat, but Susan seemed absorbed in her Navy lieutenant. At the core of her own tranquillity, Celia's mind nibbled interestedly away at a random question posed by Paul Vestry in the pursuit of one of his hobbies: "You wouldn't be one of the Baltimore Bretts, by any chance? The English branch of the family?"

That was a concept which might be worth looking into, later. At close to 2 A.M., Celia was about to get into bed, sure that all danger had passed, when a light tap at her door turned out to be Susan, ostensibly in search of a match although she must have been aware that Celia didn't smoke.

"Oh, well, have to go downstairs, I guess," Susan said lightly. "Tonight was fun, wasn't it? Mary Ellen was on top of the world—but then she would be, the year's nearly up, and it's so much nicer to be able to announce an engagement than keep it under wraps, don't you think? Or didn't you know—about David's first wife?"

Celia could only gaze, and shake her head.

"She died of meningitis last January—in fact, David and Mary Ellen first met at the hospital, and I suppose the fact that they were both so suddenly—bereaved . . ." Susan turned the unlit cigarette in her fingers. "The Mac-Intoshes are real Scottish sticklers, and David didn't want to upset them by having an engagement made public before what they consider the proper period of mourning is up, even though the marriage wasn't all that good. I suppose there's something to be said for that point of view, even when two people are so much in love with each other. Although I do think," said Susan, her gray gaze lifting and holding Celia's directly, "that it's almost tempting Fate when a girl like Mary Ellen depends so much on a man that her whole existence hangs on it." The cigarette broke with a soft snap. "Which it does, but of course living with Mary Ellen you'd know that."

"I'm sure everything will work out," said Celia politely.

And, for her and for the moment, it did. She and Mary Ellen left the next day to return to New York, and Mrs. Vestry said of the Christmas candle as fondly as her roughened voice would permit, "You must come and claim it, Celia, as soon as you can give it, as you said, a happy home."

But long before any such eventuality could come to pass, a Susan stone-faced with grief had seized the candlestick, smashed the silvery heads of the trumpet-blowing angels against a corner of the house, and flung the ruined stump into the trash.

Eleven

One of them was out here now in Santa Fe, over that spread of years and miles, to destroy her. Might even be here in the hotel, which she would leave tomorrow for the wedding toward which her whole life had been aimed.

No one was going to stop that.

Still standing, as rigid as she had been while she watched the ashes flush away forever, Celia sent her mind back on a cold and ranging hunt. It found only three faces that mattered: Mrs. Cannon's, Susan Vestry's, Willis Lambert's.

One of them had seen her, obviously, and followed her, to know that she was registered in this hotel. But wouldn't she have recognized—? No. Quite apart from the natural alterations of time, wigs were commonplace among women, and in a skiing community both sexes, whether they ever went near the slopes or not, were apt to wear outsize dark glasses which made an effective disguise in themselves.

The terrifying thing was the anonymity with which her

destruction could be accomplished. All it would take was a telephone call: "Did you know that your bride-to-be is the daughter of immigrants, with a family still living in a tenement? At least she'll manage her servants well, she was one herself for years. . . ."

Celia had no illusions as to the result of such a call. She clenched her hands, drawing a leap of light from the big emerald-cut diamond, and the savage contact of nails against palms half-stirred a memory of having done exactly that on some occasion years ago. She straightened her fingers mechanically, started to reach for the phone, thought better of it.

But there was a way; there had to be. What was the military-tactics term that kept cropping up in the newspapers? Search and destroy . . .

Twelve

The trade-paper photograph of Celia with her hair blowing bore fruit right after the Christmas weekend at the Vestrys'. Long hair was beginning to make inroads on the current chopped-off look, catching a good many models at an awkward stage, and a shampoo manufacturer was not illogically captivated by all that abundance. At a midtown studio, with a solemnity which would not have disgraced the unveiling of an entirely new concept from Detroit, Celia was posed at perhaps fifty angles, lit by and studied under varying colors and combinations of lights; had her pale hair brushed, combed, tousled, blown upon, dampened, draped through her fingers, arranged by someone else's hands strand by strand.

What ultimately appeared in one of her revered magazines was a three-quarters back view of Celia against the misty mirrored image of a man's face, showing only a curve of cheekbone, a fringe of artfully colored eyelashes attached for the occasion, and the silky torrent of hair. Although the photograph was cut off at the sweep of her

107

bare shoulders, below which she was modestly clad in a pinned-together towel, it gave a surprising impression of total nudity.

Meanwhile, whenever he could manage it safely and secretly, Celia was seeing David MacIntosh.

That he was essentially weak, and had the lost and embattled air of a man who has intended to order tomato juice and finds himself asking for a martini instead, did not bother her at all. Just as a mountain climber does not wish to rent or settle down on any of the peaks he adds to his credit, Celia had no permanent use for Mary Ellen's unofficial fiancé. He was an achievement—and an attractive one even, or especially, torn by guilt as he was. With a detachment made possible by the lack of any emotional involvement, Celia knew that he was enthralled for the moment only because she was something outside his experience.

Toward the end of January, when the hypothetical year to satisfy David's parents was up, Mary Ellen asked Celia for a sleeping pill.

From her elaborate offhandedness, it was something she had been contemplating and fighting against for some time, even though the faint lilac under her eyes would have seemed to indicate a weariness that had no need of barbiturates for assuagement. It was a sleety Sunday night, and she had just come back from dinner with David before his plane for Providence.

"Certainly," said Celia without comment, and got the little bottle from her bathroom and tipped out a capsule.

Mary Ellen studied the small yellow and white cylinder on her palm. "Thanks. Are these awfully hard to get? I mean," she said rapidly, "is it a nuisance for you to part with this one?"

"Not at all. I don't take them that often." The sleeping pills had been part of Mr. Tomlinson's supply, before he had stopped needing them, but there was no reason why Mary Ellen had to know that. "They're prescription, of course."

"Yes, I imagined they were." Mary Ellen closed her fingers thoughtfully over the capsule. "Are you and—are you in love with David?" she inquired with sudden and terrible candor. "If you are, I ought to let you know that I don't think I'm capable of bowing out gracefully. I do love him very much, and I'm pretty sure he loves me. Basically, I mean," she added with no change of tone whatever.

So someone had seen them together, even in one of the carefully out-of-the-way places where David took her . . . If Celia had been a girl to use even mental profanity, she would have used it then. As it was, she controlled her sharp anger at David, who should have had the wit to reassure this diminutive big-eyed creature. She was not by any means ready to leave the comfortable apartment for another, or even—yet—to step out from under the equally comfortable cloak of Mary Ellen's undeniably nice connections.

She said with coolness, "You're not running a fever, by any chance?" while her mind sped, assembling dates and opportunities. "The funny thing is that David is worried about *you*. Your health, that is. He doesn't want to alarm you, but he doesn't think you've been looking well, and knowing how you feel about doctors he's been sounding me out about getting you to go to one."

It was not very good, but it was the best Celia could

do with no warning at all, and it contained a tiny element of truth: after her ineradicable experience with morphine, Mary Ellen avoided doctors with the diligence other people used to dodge disease.

"How silly. I'm perfectly fine," she said, and although from her tone she might have accepted this explanation of one or more unmentioned meetings between Celia and David her gray glance held, for a moment, not its usual vague luminosity but something of the cool clarity of Susan's.

Susan, who had put David on the proscribed list after the country club dance, and who had had in her possession, however briefly, an envelope bearing the name and address of Celia's family.

In the morning, in the thoughtful way of someone checking fire exits in a building although there has been no immediate smell of smoke, Celia took a train to Bridgeport.

Her deepening dread as she approached 1000 Grand Street—that ruinously memorable address, which had been the source of only half-friendly gibes in high school—seemed to underline the necessity for this mission. While Celia herself had contrived an entirely new shell, the street was as pitilessly unchanged as an ugly old photograph. There were the same patches of dirty ice on the cracked pavements, the same bleary shop windows sandwiched in occasionally among the flaking yellow brick buildings. Factory grit and scraps of litter still came blasting around corners, borne on a wind which carried hopelessness like an aroma.

An instinctive wariness rather than any kind of delicacy

had kept Celia from wearing her leopard coat; it would stand out like a beacon in this neighborhood. The morning was too cold for doorway or lamp-post loitering, and the few faces that she saw were the dark-eyed, heavy-featured faces from childhood but unfamiliar and indifferent. Illogically, it occurred to her to hope that after all these years her family might have moved to some untraceable quarter. She had been careful never to put a return address on her own curt communications ever since leaving the Stevenson house; for all she knew, they could be reposing in a dead-letter office somewhere.

The hope was short lived. When Celia pressed the bell marked "Janitor" at the bottom of a short flight of steps at the rear of the ground-floor passage, there was the sound of a sharp slap and a child's tears, and then the door was opened by a harassed-looking young girl who looked at Celia standing there in her cinnamon coat and said ingratiatingly, "It's my chest again, Miss. Ma said I should stay home from school until my cough is better."

She looked again, and her eyes widened uncertainly. She said in a tentative voice, "Celia?"

Her sister Lena. Seven when Celia had seen her last, now promoted to minding a small niece while the mother went out to work, and, from the ironing board and heaped basket behind her, earning her own keep as well. Celia's tiny flash of pity was swallowed up in a cold revulsion: when you stepped into quicksand, it was keeping your own head above the surface that mattered.

When it became apparent that there was no one else at home or apt to arrive immediately, Celia accepted a cup of tea and inquired matter-of-factly about her parents. Her father was dead, Lena said—pneumonia, last year—

and her mother had a kitchen job at Handel's Bakery. Joseph had taken over the janitorial duties at this and the next building which gave them the apartment rent-free. Rose, the next youngest to Celia and evidently, from Lena's perfunctory nod, the mother of the child who had given up wailing in favor of staring, was working in a motel.

Celia wasn't really interested, but she heard Lena out before she asked casually, "What about Stan? Is he keeping out of trouble?"

Because Stan was her lever—and from the flash of alarm in Lena's eyes, plus the fact that she hadn't mentioned her brother, the lever would work. Although Celia was not aware of it, many large families had a Stan, a kind of professional black sheep about whom, no matter how undeservedly and thanklessly, protection closes as firmly as covered wagons forming a circle against Indians. At fifteen, Stan had been put on probation by a juvenile court for stealing car accessories; from what Celia remembered of him he would by now have discovered some far more sophisticated ploy.

"Stan's *fine*," said Lena with anxious emphasis, and hastened off the subject with the baldness of thirteen. "What are you doing, Celia? You look good."

The tone more than the words brought Celia aware of something she hadn't taken sufficient notice of in her absorption of leading up to Stan. From the outset, her sister had been regarding her with wonder and admiration, taking a close index of the good perfume, the gloves laid down with the handbag, the smoothly wound hair which wasn't, in accordance with neighborhood custom, peroxided or laquered or tormented into a great hump.

112

Lena was, in fact, giving her the wistfully devouring attention she might have accorded a picture in a movie magazine—and mightn't this be put to use?

Celia didn't answer her directly. Instead, with the pensive air she had used to threaten Mr. Tomlinson, she said, "I think you're old enough to trust, Lena."

Lena looked at once sly and important, and the child on the cot began to suck its thumb in a captivated fashion. Even a cockroach came out to listen.

"Where I work, there's a man whose wife is out to make trouble for me," said Celia, improvising rapidly and leaving Lena's thirteen-year-old imagination to make what it could of this nebulous statement. "What she'd really like to do is take me to court, so I have to go away for a while."

At the word "court" a whole procession of faceless people whom Celia's family feared with a blind instinctive fervor seemed to clump through the room—truant officers, welfare workers, probation authorities, policemen.

"She might have private detectives come here. A woman, even," said Celia, "and if they couldn't find me they'd make whatever trouble they could for the rest of you. Especially Stan." This shot was accurate; Lena paled. "So the only safe thing, and you'd better tell Mother and the others, is to say that they've got the wrong address and you never heard of me. Have you got that straight?"

The cockroach scuttled away, having found nothing with its waving feelers, the spellbound child began to fall asleep around its thumb. Lena said transfixedly, "Yes, okay, gosh, I'm glad you warned us. Don't worry," she said kindly at a sudden sharp turn of her sister's head, "it's only a rat. Where will you go, when you go away?"

For Celia had stood, mission accomplished, unable to

bear this miasma a moment longer. "California," she said crisply, buttoning her coat. "If I get a job there you'll hear from me."

It occurred to her that it might be prudent to seal this pact—if pact it was; everything depended on the depth of the communal fear for, or possibly of, Stan. Even at sixteen his temper had been something to reckon with. Celia suggested that Lena must have a birthday coming up soon, tendered a five-dollar bill, and left. A battered skateboard in the hall was the only menace she encountered between there and the station, but it was not until the train was moving that she allowed herself to believe that she had accomplished a final, scissoring snip.

She half-expected to be asked for a sleeping pill again that night, but although she woke and heard Mary Ellen moving quietly about in the small hours, the request did not come. Celia pondered this; she had assumed, from the other girl's fiercely adamant air on the evening of the headache, that the first opiate to an ex-addict was as fatal as the first drink to a true alcoholic.

She kept a curious eye on Mary Ellen for the next week or two, but the bookshop was taking inventory and it was sometimes nine thirty before her roommate got home, which would account for her pallor and the newly sharp definition of her face. Nor did Celia attach much importance to a small incident which took place the first week in March, when, a modeling appointment having been canceled, she returned to the quiet apartment in midmorning through a dark streaming rain and was just in time to answer the telephone.

"Miss Vestry, please," said a brusque male voice.

"You can reach her at the Mulberry Bookshop. The

num—"

"This *is* the Mulberry Bookshop," retorted the telephone, and clicked off.

Mary Ellen would not have been the first person to plead indisposition if it seemed the only way to get a day off, but Celia thought she had better mention the call that evening.

"I know. I went in to work after I got out of the doctor's. See, I took your advice after all," said Mary Ellen with a faint smile. "Do you want to bother with that chicken stuff for dinner or should we just settle for cube steak?"

That was evidently all she wanted to say on the subject, and Celia did not pursue the matter. There was no mystery as to why she had kept the doctor's appointment from the bookshop; with her own private intelligence service there, Mrs. Vestry would have descended immediately at this threat to her darling's health. As it was, she telephoned that same night. Celia listened with scorn to Mary Ellen's side of the exchange.

"Oh, not really sick, Mother, for heaven's sake—I do wish Miss Egan wouldn't harass everybody like this. Just a sore throat I thought I'd nurse for a couple of hours, and it's fine now . . . Yes, it's raining here too but of *course* I have an umbrella. I do take vitamins. Yes, I will . . . I will . . . I will."

Her back was to Celia as she hung up, but a mirror on the opposite wall caught the brief tight gesture of hands pressed against her small reflected face for an instant. Then she turned and said unnecessarily, "There's an old friend of my mother's, Maude Egan, who lives around the corner from the shop and has nothing to do but read. She comes in at least once a day—taking me under her wing, I suppose she calls it—and then files her reports. If for any reason I'm not there, like this morning, or I *am* there and have no fresh news of—"

Color rushed drivenly into her face and she stopped short with an effect of biting her tongue. Then, as though she could dispel the clear unspoken echo of David's name, she said abruptly, "I'm going to take a long hot bath. Let's just let the dishes go to hell tonight, shall we?" and withdrew.

Almost anyone else in Celia's position, faced with such unusual behavior, would have inquired whether the doctor had said anything that morning to upset Mary Ellen. Celia merely gazed speculatively after her.

Queried on the subject, she would have given the opinion that no semiofficial engagement could remain in that suspended state for long; that it would either reach the expected conclusion or fall apart completely. Now she realized with faint surprise that Mary Ellen, without tears or recriminations or any other display, had succeeded in maintaining the status quo far beyond the predictable point of dissolution.

Moreover, she would ultimately win. Celia had learned a good deal about David MacIntosh's character and she knew, even if he didn't at the moment, that although he wanted her now it was Mary Ellen whom he wanted in the long run. At their last meeting he had implored Celia to spend a weekend with him at an inn in Providence, but afterwards he would be quite capable of guilt, self-abasement, and the declaration that they—because Celia would be included in this sweeping judgment—were not fit to kiss the ground which Mary Ellen Vestry walked upon.

Things must certainly not be allowed to reach that

stage. And here Celia's mind informed her of what must have been nearing the surface for some time: if it had been a triumph to take David away from Mary Ellen, how much more triumphant to hand him back—to have him in her own gift, so to speak?

But Celia, sitting on the couch while bath water ran distantly and traffic swished by in the wet street below, had made one of the few serious miscalculations of her new life. Three days later, there was nobody to hand David back to. There was only the diminishing wail of a siren and, in the lobby near the door, a small, narrow, black kid slipper.

Thirteen

Mary Ellen Vestry's death was reduced to a brief inside-page item in the newspapers, choicer space being reserved for the suicides who teetered on ledges or set themselves on fire or slaughtered their whole families prior to the act. There was nothing bizarre or even very unusual about a self-administered overdose of sleeping pills and a suicide note; the contents of the note were not revealed but the account stated, or understated, that the victim had been "despondent."

The body had been discovered at 4 P.M. by a family friend (the ubiquitous Maude Egan). Celia's name as roommate did not appear at all.

After her first shock, and a tiny trickle of personal fear, Celia was indignant. Suicide seemed to her scandalous, in somewhat the same category as wandering out from showers with no clothes on; and on top of that she had been accused of murder by a Susan Vestry almost unrecognizably wild with grief. Susan did not make the accusation until the door of the apartment had finally closed behind the police—not from consideration, Celia knew, but a desire to shield Mary Ellen as much as possible from the eyes of strangers.

The suicide note had been taken away as evidence, but in the confusion of Maude Egan's hysterics and the arrival of the finally located Susan, someone had let drop the gist of it: that Mary Ellen was sorry, but "she could not go through it again." Susan, queried by the police as to the meaning of this, had a choice of two betrayals: she could say that fifteen months ago her sister had lost a fiancé in a fatal accident and had just now been in the process of losing to another woman the man she hoped to marry, or she could explain the period of morphine addiction and Mary Ellen's terror of a recurrence.

Out of feminine solidarity she chose the latter, and the almost empty bottle of pills which had anchored the note, and which from its date Mary Ellen had clearly obtained as a result of her visit to a doctor three days earlier, was also borne away as evidence. Susan said to the younger of the departing policemen, "Will they have to—You know what she took and why. Will they still . . . ?"

The policeman understood. "Well, yes. Just routine," he said kindly, as though this made the fact of an autopsy less painful. "They'll let you know when you can . . . they'll let you know."

And that was when the apartment door closed. Susan picked up Mary Ellen's huge calf handbag and put it down quickly, looking distraught. Her bewildered glance about her said that when a member of the family had been taken away in an ambulance it was usual to pack at least a few things to bring to the hospital—but Mary Ellen would never need anything again.

Susan had washed her face at some point, in the calmly irrational way in which such things are done in the middle of catastrophe, and her eyes looked dry and glittery and stretched apart. She said slowly to Celia, "You dreadful creature. You killed her, but I suppose you know that."

Celia chose to misinterpret the charge. "When I left here this morning and she wasn't up yet, I knocked at her door and she called that she was going in to work a little late. How could I have known that she was going to—"

Susan brushed this aside. "You knew about that ghastly accident, when Tom Anders was killed." It was the first time anyone had ever told Celia his name. "You knew what that did to Mary Ellen, physically and every other way. You knew that she loved David desperately, because he was the one who put her back together again more than anybody else, and you waded right in and took *that* to pieces."

"David is a perfectly free—"

"David is a fool," said Susan bitterly, "but so is almost any man when a woman flings herself at him as openly as you did. Oh, I watched you at Christmas. He simply didn't know what had struck him, and Mary Ellen was so damn trusting—" Her voice began to shake and thicken, and her eyes to fill; she dashed at them furiously with the back of her wrist. "Dear *God*, to think that I once walked down those stairs with you and said I thought you'd be good for her . . ."

She turned her suddenly blinded gaze away, pretending to hunt for her handbag. Celia said with an assumption of dignity, "I realize that you're very upset and you're saying things—"

"*Upset?*" repeated Susan wildly, wheeling on her. "You

mean just because my sister is dead and my mother has collapsed? What would make you think a thing like that?"

For a terrible instant she seemed about to lose all control, and then she sent an unrecognizing glance around the room and returned to her almost equally frightening, recitative calm. "There'll be someone here tomorrow to— take things away, and I hope to God you're out. The service will be private, and don't come near it or any of us in any way. I wouldn't be responsible."

Whatever Celia's rage at this echo of dismissal, it did not seem the moment to remind Susan that she paid half the rent here. She packed a bag and went to the Hotel Alexandra, where she explained casually to Mrs. Pond that her apartment was being repainted. That was always a bore, observed Mrs. Pond, but how nice it was to see her again.

And, although even a few months had tended to diminish the hotel and its social director in her eyes, Celia was glad to be back. For the moment the Alexandra was a talisman place, her previous connection with it unknown to Willis Lambert, his face suffused with hatred on the station concourse, or to vindictive Mrs. Cannon, or to Susan Vestry with her look of naked ferocity.

It was fortunate—more than fortunate under the circumstances—that Celia had made that trip to Bridgeport.

At the time, her vision had contained a resentful Susan, angry on her sister's behalf, taking the trouble to track down that elementary address and returning, triumphant, to report that Brett was not the name Celia had been born with; that her mother and the rest of them were very much alive in a wretched little basement apartment, although

121

she had not troubled to visit them for years; that she had left them originally to go into service as a maid. Not that there was anything wrong with being a maid, Susan would undoubtedly have pointed out in her high-minded Vestry fashion; what mattered was that Celia had turned her back on her family and lied about herself from start to finish.

All that would have been disastrous enough. But, in the new light of the terrible, inexcusable thing Mary Ellen had done to herself, Susan would not have been content to stop there. She would have traced Celia from the Stevensons' to the Strykers' and—armed with Mrs. Cannon's name—to Stedman Circle, where it would have been simple to discover old Mr. Tomlinson's death as the result of a fall and Celia's inheritance of the property.

Celia reminded herself coolly that she had not touched Mr. Tomlinson, but she was well aware that it could be made to look . . . that Susan could do her considerable harm. Particularly in the unlikely event that she matched notes with Mrs. Cannon.

But none of it was going to happen. As a result of the trip to Bridgeport and the talk with Lena, her family would disavow any knowledge of a Celia, out of simple—and simple-minded—fear.

And yet there was a tiny flaw somewhere in what should have been Celia's total relief at having sealed off that threat. Something she had said, or not said, to her sister? Or some physical object in that dreary, cluttered room? She frowned unconsciously at the somewhat worn carpeting of Mrs. Pond's room, where they were having a late highball, and Mrs. Pond studied her with the acuteness that lay behind her misty-looking green eyes. "You've got something more on your mind than an apartment painting," she observed without archness; anything in that vein was husbanded for her labors in the Alexandra's public rooms. "A man, possibly?"

"More or less." It was a lie; Celia had not thought once about David MacIntosh since walking into that horrible scene with the police and weeping Maude Egan and Susan and the door standing nakedly wide on the silence of Mary Ellen's bedroom. Now she gave him a moment of fierce concentration. Was it possible that out of shock and remorse he would babble something that a newspaper might consider worth printing, something that would drag in Celia's name? On the whole—a man who deferred to his parents' sensibilities to the extent David had—no. Still, Celia was sharply alarmed that she had overlooked this potential menace; for a few seconds, the world seemed to contain nothing but enemies.

"Which usually means more," Mrs. Pond was remarking thoughtfully. She tipped her dark head, to which she had recently added a swash of disarmingly false pink-gold; the part of Celia which was always clinically detached noted that this was the kind of thing women like Mrs. Pond could do with casual success. "You know, I did think when you arrived that you were looking a trifle edgy."

Celia glanced at her with coolness.

"But then, March is a month you can have, for all of me. Wherever you are," said Mrs. Pond, suddenly pensive over some problem of her own, "it's the perfect time to be somewhere else."

To be somewhere else . . . It was an almost uncanny reflection of Celia's growingly restive frame of mind.

She would have been both angry and incredulous if

123

someone had suggested that she was not unlike a forced laboratory growth which was able to seek out a host plant, feed to satiation, drop off and roam in search of another host for its supply of a different element. But she did recognize that she had absorbed all that the world of the Vestrys could give her.

It was a comfortable and decorative world, but there was no place in it for the kind of niche Celia planned for herself. She would have slipped away from the Vestrys soon even without the awkwardness of Mary Ellen's suicide, because almost without conscious effort on her part a diagram was taking shape in her mind.

She lay awake for a long time that night, aware, as she had been months before upon first moving to the Alexandra, that whatever move she made now would be of extreme importance. In a way, this plan would be like going back to Square One in a child's game—but from it she could take a giant step.

She presented herself the next morning in Mrs. Pond's blond-wood-and-lime office and proposed that, in return for room and board, she be taken on as assistant to the social director.

Mrs. Pond had been in the hotel business too long to register surprise at anything. She gazed across her desk at Celia's well-groomed energy and then nodded at the little cubbyhole that opened off one wall. "I do have Miriam, you know, for typing and errands and the phone."

It was said as crisply and sensibly as though Mrs. Pond, after hours, had not complained irritably about Miriam's dumpiness, prattling, and general inefficiency, and Celia responded in kind. "Yes, I know, but there are other things

I could take off your hands, although I can type too if things get rushed. I could help with the fashion shows"— for some reason Mrs. Pond had an almost pathological hatred for the hotel's occasional fashion shows—"and the children's parties, and I'd consider the training as payment."

Mrs. Pond's phone burred then and she lifted the receiver, but she went on gazing at Celia reflectively as she talked; Celia, in turn, felt far more tense than she had under Charlotte Wise's clever, protuberant dark eyes. Mrs. Pond hung up and made a note on a pad. She said, "Well, we can hardly have unsalaried employees—it's against all kinds of laws, for one thing—but I suppose there *is* room in here for another desk, and I'll speak to Mr. Tashman."

Mr. Tashman was the personnel manager, a grim little tyrant who, according to Mrs. Pond's unguarded statements, stalked about with his hands clasped behind his back seeing which of the staff was superfluous that day. Celia's heart sank, and lifted again as Mrs. Pond said with a slight smile "—and Mr. Wilhelm.

Mr. Wilhelm was the assistant manager of the hotel, and the author of the flowers which were usually to be seen in Mrs. Pond's room. Celia left the office in a hopeful frame of mind which was justified at ten thirty that night, when the social director tapped at her door to say, "As of tomorrow, you'll get sixty a week and a room on the seventh floor. I'll work you to the bone, I warn you."

"Good," Celia said, and meant it.

"Oh, and one thing." The friendliness of Mrs. Pond's voice and eyes did not alter in the least. "No throat-cutting, hm? Well, poor Miriam's, if you must, but on no account mine . . . I imagine you'll have to do something

125

about your apartment," she added in the same light and practical tone while Celia was still gazing in assumed bewilderment, "so why don't you take the morning for that?"

. . . The morning. Mary Ellen Vestry was being buried out on Long Island; Celia assured herself of that by a glance at the obituary column (services private, interment in Oak Memorial Park) before she set out for the apartment. In the vestibule she glanced from habit at the mailbox, where a new slip saying only "Brett, C." had been inserted, and took out a single envelope with her name and address typed on the front. It was postmarked Providence.

There was no one in the shadowed lobby. Celia tore the envelope open, and read David's brief and frantic-looking handwriting which said, without salutation, "I must see you. Will be in N.Y. Friday night and phone from airport."

Coolly, without even having to think about it, Celia screwed paper and envelope into a single tight twist, thrust it deep into the urn of sand beside the elevator, and went up to the apartment with the big suitcase borrowed from Mrs. Pond.

And they—Susan or an emissary—had been very quick indeed, because in spite of what had been done the air had had time to go still and dead again. Through the wide-standing door Mary Ellen's vivid and cluttered room was now a shell containing bed and bureau. The door to Celia's bedroom was closed. She paused just inside the long living room and looked about her with cold and mounting rage.

The apartment in which she had the right to live for

two more weeks if she chose could still have been called furnished, technically, although the Navajo rugs were gone and the superintendent had not gotten around to putting back whatever floor covering they had replaced. The couch and chairs and some of the lamps were still there, and so was the bookcase—now empty except for a meticulous pile of Celia's magazines—and it would have been possible to cook in the kitchen. But every trace of warmth and charm had been remorselessly stripped away: the rooms had the sullen chill of a landscape just before a storm.

To herself, in her frozen wrath, Celia put down to greed this total removal of everything that Mary Ellen had brought to this place where she had taken her own life. With rapid contempt, because that was the only way to dispel the impression that she was being evicted, she swept the bathroom shelves clean of her possessions, folded her clothes into the suitcases augmented by Mrs. Pond's, and was ringing the superintendent's bell only a little more than an hour later.

The superintendent had clearly been interrupted at his coffee break, and by the time he joined Celia at the elevator to go up for her bags a well-dressed young couple had entered the lobby. They had the tentative, appraising air of people who had come to look at an apartment with a view to renting, although Celia knew that there were no vacancies. She did not miss the surreptitious and sidelong glance the superintendent shot at her before he said to them, "I'll be right with you folks, soon as I get this lady's bags."

The lease had been in Mary Ellen's name and terminated automatically with her death, Celia supposed, but what right had this man, this employee, to assume without even asking that she could not afford to keep the apartment on by herself? She let a little of her fury escape; she said to the waiting couple as the elevator doors opened, "I know it's a silly superstition, not being able to bear an apartment where there's been a suicide, but I just can't help myself," and had the satisfaction of seeing the smiles congeal.

Stonily, mouth tight with anger, the superintendent carried Celia's bags down through the now-empty lobby to the curb, stonily accepted her key, said, "You want to leave a forwarding address?"

"I'll leave it at the post office." Celia held out the dollar bill she had marshalled from her handbag; direct tipping, and not the coins left anonymously on a restaurant tray, was still new enough to give her a tiny sense of patronage. "Here you are."

"Keep it," said the superintendent contemptuously, gazing Celia fully in the face. "I wouldn't want you to run yourself low on my account." He added over his shoulder with disproportionate savagery as he walked away, "Think you're smart."

But Celia had recovered her equanimity, and she did not allow this startling little unpleasantness to ruffle it. The March sunlight had a thin, windy, exciting look; she was not only embarked upon the course she wanted but was being paid for it; by her bald reference to suicide she had wiped away that humiliating sense of eviction. As always when she had cut any unpleasant ties, all was well in Celia's world.

It was uncharacteristic of her to have forgotten the buried sharpness of something overlooked in that visit to the basement apartment in Bridgeport. Fresh preoccupations had covered it like skin healing over a thorn, and there was no way of knowing that it would come piercing through, carrying a killing infection with it, years later on a cold New Mexico night.

Fourteen

Celia was Mrs. Pond's assistant for nearly a year. By the end of the first month the hapless Miriam was replaced by a stenographer-typist who came in for two hours every morning, and Celia's salary could be raised accordingly. She looked upon the extra money as a fringe benefit; when she had told Mrs. Pond that she would regard the training as payment, she had meant it more sincerely than the other woman could guess.

Mrs. Pond was extremely astute at her job, which necessarily overlapped into other of the hotel's functions, and Celia's attention to learning was as eager as a sponge. Mindful of the light but crisp admonition against throat-cutting, she stayed in the background at first, dealing with routine chores and being meticulously businesslike from the moment she entered the office in the morning. She never advanced new ideas, for the simple reason that she hadn't any, but could often, because of her domestic training, find practical short cuts in Mrs. Pond's.

Gradually, she took on slightly more important tasks. She dealt with outside caterers when there was an unexpected clash and the hotel kitchens were busy; she interviewed purveyors of puppet shows and other diversions for the young residents of the Alexandra; she occasionally filled in for Mrs. Pond at such activities. She found out the lowest price for which a ballroom could be decorated with flowers without looking like a rural high-school dance, and absorbed by osmosis how much chicken à la king and patty shells and peas, preceded by fruit salad supreme and followed by coffee and petits fours, would be needed to stoke a banquet of shoe buyers.

She substituted occasionally in the fashion shows, and she did the preliminary screening for the monthly amateur nights which were one of Mrs. Pond's prime headaches. ("*Why* will mothers think fat nine-year-olds look fetching in tutus? Why are people allowed to roam about at will, playing harmonicas?")

And all the time, Celia learned. Like a person with extraordinary peripheral vision, she took in far more than she realized.

She became able to sense, as many women never did, the moment when a mood—at a convention or birthday party or anniversary celebration—was going flat or, worse, turning bellicose. There wasn't always something to be done about it: "A Jolly Good Fellow" might fall on sullen ears, and an enormous candlelit cake be greeted with silent derision, but it was a valuable thing to know. So was the average number of cocktails needed to oil any adult function. Two, decided Celia; one left people resentful about the stinginess of the affair and three always had a few indiscretions burbled into the wrong ear.

For her own purposes, perhaps the most important skill she acquired was the ability to see as a whole any social function of a public nature. It might look impossibly daunting, but it could be broken down into a number of quite tidy parts which meshed at the end without a seam showing. Although Celia was not aware of it then, this faculty was one which highly educated, far more intelligent women than she often could not master in a lifetime.

Inevitably, she was thrown into contact with a good many people for the first time in her life. Being without humor, she would never be a participant in the light, fast give-and-take around her, but she had the possibly more valuable gift of realizing her limitations; this gave her a removed and reflective air, as if there were all sorts of witty contributions she might make if she felt like it.

Some of the people she met were like images springing out of a scrapbook kept in Celia's head: slender, beautifully groomed women who were fifty and looked forty, busied themselves with smart charities and cropped up in the society sections of the Sunday papers. Celia learned not to be cowed by them even when, making arrangements for a benefit luncheon, they called her "Sweetie," which she discovered was a mask for upper-level feminine irritation. She also learned unconsciously to preface her own exclamations, so that she greeted good news with "But how marvelous!" and the other kind with "But how ghastly."

One such woman was Mrs. Horace P. Dillworth, "Cricket" to Vogue and her other intimates, and it was through Mrs. Dillworth that, not quite a year after she had started working at the Alexandra, Celia became an associate coordinator for the League for America's Deprived Youth. Or, as its stationery indicated chastely, LADY.

The League was an accredited charity, receiving a tiny automatic slice of federal child-welfare funds but supported mainly by private contributions and endowments. Its executives were handsomely housed in two burgundy-and-gray floors of a midtown office building, and from some mystifying source—through caseworkers?—an actual Deprived Youth was produced and featured in a monthly newsletter which went to the League branches in Chicago and Houston.

Much to her relief, Celia never saw a flesh-and-blood waif in all her tenure there. She was well paid, with a little office of her own in which she scrupulously read newsletters about what other charities were doing and made notes which sometimes appeared in their own newsletters. Her chief duties were the decorously hounding letters which went off regularly to reliable contributors from the past ("LADY is knocking at your door again . . .") and legwork for the frequent fund-raising breakfasts and luncheons and dinners.

The staff wasn't large. There was a switchboard operator who got in a lot of reading, and two typists who coped with a vast flow of pointless correspondence. There were also two or three interchangeable-looking, just-out-of-college girls with the ink scarcely dry on their sociology degrees; a publicity man, a handsome occasional lawyer who said, perhaps truthfully, that he donated his time to the League, an office boy who had the flavor of one of the better prep schools, and a large handful of decorative women with grown children, bored husbands, and otherwise-occupied friends. These last really did donate their time and, as they were not in a position to do much harm, probably did a little random good.

Certainly the League suited them. They stayed effortlessly busy and animated all day, and in some mysterious way which Celia could not fathom, their delicately dry faces did not secrete anything as vulgar as oil; at five o'clock, only the quick whiff of a powder puff and a touch of light lipstick was required to send them on their perfumed way home.

Celia felt let into a Garden of Eden when a Mrs. Ruykendahl, with whom she had exchanged civilities in the elevator and once shared a taxi, drifted into her office with a candidly appraising air one afternoon. "I'm going to be terribly frank and say that a dinner guest has canceled out on me, and could you possibly help me out of a spot tonight? If you're not busy, of course."

In spite of her prettily deferential air Mrs. Ruykendahl clearly assumed that no young woman presented with such an invitation could be *that* busy, and she was quite right. Celia, who had a date with the publicity man, said that she'd be delighted, and Mrs. Ruykendahl bent and scribbled and said, "Seven o'clock, then, and here's the address and you're an absolute dear. We'll only be eight, and not formal."

Celia rummaged through her slender but now-good wardrobe, and wore a creamy dinner suit with the small topaz earrings Mrs. Pond had given her as a parting present. She was dazzled at the Ruykendahl residence, and not in the least dismayed that she had been invited as partner for a fortyish man with thinning corn-colored hair and prominent teeth. She was composed and quiet, but the circumstances gave her a glow not to be observed among the other women present; she did not miss her hostess's occasional glance of approbation.

No one, looking at Celia, would have suspected that her whole body echoed with triumph and excitement. She had served at so many dinners that, presently, the array of heavy Ruykendahl silver and crystal held no bafflements for her, and she had so completely mastered the art of taking in detail that, to the outward eye, these might have been her natural surroundings. She was neither coy nor vivacious, as either attitude would sit awkwardly upon someone with her height and boning and breadth of shoulder, and this alone was challenging to her partner, who was not only wealthy but eligible.

He began to draw her out. Had she perhaps, he inquired, been to school in England as a child? He was sure he had noticed an inflection now and again . . .

"Yes, people tell me that. It's very simple really," said Celia, smiling and unobtrusively laying down her fork; she had prepared her groundwork well, but she was not going to cope with it and broccoli in Hollandaise sauce at the same time. "When I was quite little I spent some time, summers and school vacations, with cousins of my mother's in Baltimore. They were English, or rather my Uncle Harry was—he wasn't my uncle, but of course I called him that—in fact there was a title somewhere," said Celia, throwing this out with democratic vagueness. "Anyway, nothing would do but an English governess for their children, and as I was about the same age I got the benefit of the accent too. I sometimes think I hang onto it subconsciously," she turned her dark gaze on him with disarming

135

candor "simply out of nostalgia."

Her partner, with no difficult paths to tread, was disposing of his broccoli without any diminution of attentiveness. "You've never been back, then?"

"No." Perhaps because of her peculiar excitement Celia was ravenously hungry, and she now judged it safe to pick up her fork again. As a result of Paul Vestry's random inquiry on that Christmas weekend, she had paid fifty dollars to a cynical-eyed man in a third-floor walk-up office who provided wanted family trees, and she felt tranquil. "Uncle Harry died, and the children were taken back to his family in England. I've lost all touch, but I believe the old place in Baltimore has changed hands at least twice. I'd really rather not see it at all."

"Sad," observed her partner, dispatching a last piece of roast beef.

"Oh, well." A rapid under-the-lashes glance around the table convinced Celia that she would have to abandon the rest of her own roast beef, as the middle-aged maid had been standing patiently in the background for some time. "What's really important is to recognize the especially happy parts of childhood while you're having them, isn't it?"

This poignant philosophy came straight out of a LADY newsletter, and was strangely unanswerable. Celia consumed her dessert and coffee relaxedly and with enjoyment. She had never read the advice of a celebrated fashion authority that any new costume should be worn first in solitude, so as to guarantee ease on the part of the wearer, but the effect of her own experiment was much the same.

She had tried on the Baltimore-Bretts costume, and could don it without worry.

136

Her dinner partner escorted her home at eleven, pressed her hand warmly, said decorously, "May I?" and kissed her cheek with unexpected expertise. Celia never saw him again, because he was only traveling through New York on some business mission connected with Mr. Ruykendahl's shipping interests, but for her the evening had been an unqualified success. Almost by accident she had hit upon the only social role she could carry off. She might not sparkle, but she could certainly glow; she could create a tiny intriguing island of silence, full of what appeared to be thoughtfully withheld comment.

And—unable to go to bed in her tense exhilaration, Celia paced about, occasionally pausing to study her mirrored reflection for nearly a minute at a time—she would have to educate herself in a new area; the evening had shown her that. Other women would challenge her, even if men did not, so although she found any reading matter apart from fashion magazines both difficult and boring, she would have to familiarize herself to some extent with the national news. Politics she felt she could safely ignore, but it was necessary to know something (she could just read the reviews) about best-selling novels and talked-about plays. In total seriousness, Celia decided to set apart an hour for this every night, or perhaps an hour and a half until she began to get caught up.

In order to allay any fears Mrs. Ruykendahl might have had, Celia was even more businesslike than usual at the office the next day, but before the week was out they had shared one of the strictly one-hour lunches which was all Mrs. Ruykendahl and her cohorts allowed themselves. On the next occasion they were joined by a woman of whom Celia stood in genuine awe.

Blanca Devlin was the only real professional at the League, a fund-raiser of almost legendary accomplishment. In her late forties, she was a magnificently handsome creature—tall, swashbuckling, with a lustrous tan at all seasons of the year, engaging laugh-crinkles about amber-brown eyes in which no honest mirth ever appeared, and creamy teeth as polished as if they had just emerged from a tumbling machine.

She wore her black hair in a chignon and had her big-brimmed hats designed to accommodate it, and had been married to a well-known foreign correspondent, now an alcoholic, and a novelist who also had drinking problems. (There was some, but not much, speculation about this coincidence; Blanca would be a bad enemy.) She was on first-name terms with the segment of New York to be found in fashionable restaurants and theater lobbies, and even well-established Mrs. Ruykendahl had been known to send currying little smiles in her direction.

Blanca Devlin took a cool and somewhat sardonic liking to Celia, almost as though she had divined Celia's origins and goals at a glance and were tendering a half-mocking salute. One result was that Celia's circle of acquaintances began to widen automatically; another, that she gradually took on, like reflected light, a faint trace of the older woman's arrogance. Mrs. Devlin had this down to a fine art. Kept waiting in an outer office in spite of an appointment confirmed by telephone, there was never, for her, anything so amateurish as the glanced-at watch or the tapped foot. Instead she would draw from one of her bold handbags a small lizard notebook and a narrow gold pencil and, gazing with apparent blankness at the female behind the desk, commence making notes.

"They can't stand it," she told Celia indulgently. "No secretary is that secure."

By June, Celia had taken over the sublet of a small, pretty apartment near Gramercy Park, the normal domain of a young divorcee friend of Blanca's. She paid without a qualm a rent which would have appalled her two years earlier. She was being better paid than she had expected at LADY; she had been able to save a good part of her salary at the Hotel Alexandra; she received dividends from her investments. Most of all, she had learned to spend money only where it would pay her a return.

As it had. It was a measure of Celia's progress that she looked back in wonderment to her sense of achievement at having been sent as a possible model to a Seventh Avenue garment house—but only that far back. She was too realistic to fall into any half-daydream about her family background, but she was so at ease with her own version that she was able to do some casual embroidering. When she gave her first small cocktail party, after much reading up on the subject, she attributed her superlative little cheese puffs to the recipe of a housekeeper they had once had. "A terrible bully, really, but a heart of gold. At least we always assumed she had a heart of gold; I don't think it was ever put to the test . . ."

The shock was all the greater when the whole inherently dangerous business threatened to come crashing down around her.

Fifteen

Just as New York could narrow down to the confines of a very small town and produce when it was least wanted the rage-congested face of a Willis Lambert, it could suddenly appear to have swallowed, or spewed forth to untraceable places, every known contact with the past. On a late morning already sticky with heat, Celia had nothing more worrisome on her mind than the luncheon and fashion show being sponsored by the League and a Fifth Avenue store, invitations to which had been sent out to the store's charge customers two weeks earlier.

In spite of Mrs. Devlin's competence, there were usually last-minute, behind-the-scenes little crises which Celia was particularly good at dealing with, bringing to the job a kind of built-in calm and inventiveness. Anyone else might have been rendered helpless with mirth on many of these occasions, but Celia was proof against such dangers.

It struck nobody at the League or the store as being in the least piquant, for instance, that the fashions to be shown for wealthy young sprigs were of a kind achieved

140

effortlessly in the slums and ghettos to which, after the salaries of Mrs. Devlin and Celia and the publicity man and the earnest college girls and the lesser corps of personnel, the proceeds of the affair were directed. What one fashion magazine called "the wonderful woebegone look" was having its brief heyday, and there was not a tongue in cheek anywhere.

This particular function was running very smoothly indeed, and a few minutes before the fashion show itself was to begin Celia received from Mrs. Devlin the signaling glance that meant all was well and she could go back to the office. It was an absolute rule that a copy of the League's by-laws be at hand, in the unlikely event that anyone should ask a question about structural organization, and Celia started automatically for the table and microphone Mrs. Devlin would share with the store's commentator.

Across perhaps five yards of murmurous, mildly expectant space, she met the idly quartering eye of Mrs. Cannon.

Their glance was like a tiny clash between tiddlywink counters, with Celia having the minute advantage of overlap simply because she was on her feet and moving, while Mrs. Cannon, seated and faintly bored, needed that extra click of time to synchronize sight and recognition. Celia managed to keep walking, altering course away from the table for which she had been bound, and to turn her head casually as if a friend had waved from the other distance. Her whole body was stiff with the dread of an actual call in that iced-over voice: *"Celia?* Celia Brett?"

But it did not come. A pillar with inset panels of mirror intervened, and Celia kept it between her and a side exit until a gradual hush, and then a spatter of applause and a woman's light, clear, amplified voice, told her that the the fashion show had begun. Only then did she dare to stop and peer guardedly around a looped-back fold of pink velvet curtain.

Even from this changed perspective it wasn't difficult to locate Mrs. Cannon, shiny black head arrogantly bare in an assemblage of almost universally hatted women. She appeared to be absorbed in a model lounging down the runway in pipestem corduroys—"knotted about the waist, you'll notice, with *real rope,*" the commentator was saying in tones of charmed delight—but as Celia watched, the black head turned to one side and then the other in a combing inspection of the audience. The way in which Mrs. Cannon presently lit a cigarette had a dismissive, I-must-have-been-mistaken air.

Celia went back to the League, where her shaken appearance (she did not pale prettily) was immediately noted by one of the college girls proffering iced coffee: "It's this heat, Miss Brett—you look just *awful.*"

In her own office she reminded herself that she had been hatted and gloved in that lightning confrontation, that there was nothing to identify her with LADY, no conceivable reason why Mrs. Cannon, failing to find her in the audience, should approach Mrs. Devlin after the fashion show and say, "Your organization doesn't by any chance employ a Celia Brett—tall, blonde, in burgundy and white stripes today? . . . Well, what an absolutely weird coincidence. She was housekeeper for my uncle until his fatal accident—I'd found her as a maid, actually . . ."

The air conditioning turned Celia coldly damp. She knew all about Cinderella, and had been to see *My Fair Lady,* but she had also become acquainted with the mores of the magic circle into which she was finally beginning to winnow her way. It was acceptable to be a multiple divorcee, or to enter into a liaison without benefit of divorce if this were done with sufficient dash. Feckless heirs who were openly known to have the last piece of Faberge in and out of hock were regarded with indulgence and sympathy—in fact, vied for. Triumph over origin was given its enthusiastic due, especially at LADY: "He's an assistant producer now, if you please, and when you think that his father was a steam presser that's rather marvelous, isn't it?" but these plaudits were rendered among the insiders, like the handshake of a secret society. "Only in America" was carefully left unsaid, lest the accent come out wrong.

What these people would never forgive was a feeling of having been made fools of—not only to themselves but, far worse, to each other.

There is nothing to worry about, said Celia strengtheningly to herself. Hadn't Mrs. Cannon visibly decided to shrug the whole thing off as a startling resemblance? For that matter, and for all she knew, Celia might have married in that long interval and, there as an invited charge customer, have some entirely untraceable new name. Yes, she would think that—wouldn't she?

But it was a long afternoon. No echo of Mr. Tomlinson's despairing old voice or clutching fingers intruded, nor did any vision of the narrow black slipper that had fallen from Mary Ellen's foot when the ambulance men carried her out. Celia had only the simple and obsessive fear of someone who just *might* have slipped a self-destructive letter irretrievably into a postbox.

At four o'clock, Blanca Devlin's cut-out cartwheel of pale gold straw appeared around the doorway. "It went off very well, I thought. Come along to my office and we'll get a report off and then"— she was the only woman at the League who would have made such a frivolous suggestion —"we'll leave a bit early and reward ourselves with something long and cold."

It would have been easy, and very possibly fatal, to have been lulled then; to have argued that that shocking near-encounter with Mrs. Cannon or another enemy was hardly likely to happen again, or that even the strongest desire for revenge was apt to wither with time. Celia did not deceive herself. She had been warned, with the accuracy of a shadow projected along a wall in advance of the actuality that was casting it. In the morning, with just the right amount of regret masking her savage resentment at being driven out of this berth, she tendered her resignation.

Mrs. Cockburn, who did the hiring at LADY, was regretful too. Large, bland, dressed in a small-fortune's worth of clothes that fitted her like random slipcovers, she said, "I really am sorry. Both Mrs. Devlin and Mrs. Ruykendahl have spoken very highly of your work. If you'd been here longer we might have been able to arrange a leave of absence or some such thing, but as it is I'm afraid . . ."

Celia indicated with a smiling gesture that she hadn't expected anything of the kind. Mrs. Cockburn inspected her from burnished head to polished toe and grew almost petulant, peering over her pearls and her massive bosom at the fresh memo clipped to the personnel file. "Hasn't this—person someone else to call upon? Surely when it's a matter of your career . . ."

Celia shook her head with every appearance of ruefulness. "Apparently not, and I do feel obligated. She was so very kind during my mother's last illness."

Mrs. Cockburn, in her particular avocation, had no choice but to be struck by this display of duty: it was by no means usual in this day and age for a young woman to terminate a successful job in order to go to the side of an ailing old family friend. Indeed, it was quite singular. Walking with Celia to the door of her office, she bestowed a shoulder pat with one ringed hand. "We don't like losing you, my dear, but I do admire you. Mind you come and say good-bye to me before you leave."

Everyone else admired Celia too; there was no trenchant green-eyed Mrs. Pond in this insulated world. Blanca Devlin said that she would have no trouble in finding another interim tenant for the smart little apartment, and Mrs. Ruykendahl pressed upon Celia the addresses of and notes of introduction to two Junior League friends who had migrated to the west coast. "And you must let me give a little dinner."

Mrs. Devlin also entertained for her, a circumstance Celia would have found unimaginable a year ago but greeted now with cool pleasure, as though her adult life had been full of such events. As opposed to the stately progress of cocktails and several dinner courses at the Ruykendahls', there were bottles in profusion on a long marble-topped Italian table and a deceptively careless-looking buffet of anchovied toast, shrimp and avocado salad, ham, strong runny cheese, cold fresh fruit, paralyzingly potent coffee in elegant little red and gold cups. Of the perhaps twenty guests—to Celia's awe Blanca lapsed into rapid French with a few—the prize was an older woman who had been asked chiefly because she had just returned from a year in San Francisco.

The woman was shy, an oddity in this self-possessed gathering, and seemed flattered to be considered an authority on anything. Celia's attentiveness encouraged her to provide information on what might be expected of the climate in the next month or so, and—she was clearly unaware of the supposed reason for Celia's departure—an estimate of the apartment and job conditions. Before leaving, she wrote a few names on a piece of paper, circling the last. "A distant connection, in a complicated way," she said with peculiar deprecation, and Celia glanced politely at the paper and stowed it away with Mrs. Ruykendahl's friends.

At the end of the evening, thanking Blanca Devlin, she asked, "Who was that woman who was telling me about San Francisco, the rather elderly one in the printed chiffon?" and Blanca said carelessly, "Mrs. Hays-Faulkner. Nice, isn't she, in a wispy way? Her husband was consul in one of the Latin-American countries before he died. Jim and I knew them quite well at one time."

Jim was the newspaperman ex-husband. Celia went away impressed, and spent a few minutes before bed in what had now become a ritual inspection of herself in various attitudes before her mirror. ('Celia Brett, deep in conversation with Mrs. Hays-Faulkner, widow of . . .') *Cecelia* Brett, she thought suddenly. A tiny alteration, but perhaps a safeguard if her name should appear in a San Francisco society column. . .

With her decision to leave New York, the city became peopled immediately with frightening likenesses of Susan Vestry, Mrs. Cannon, and Willis Lambert: the wonder now seemed that one of them hadn't pursued her into

146

LADY's offices. She thought that she saw a thinner David MacIntosh in a Longchamps. More disturbing still, on a train visit to the lawyer, was a woman with a crimson mouth and black brows beetling over a blue gaze, menacingly reminiscent of Betty . . . Schirm, was it? Suspicious even all that long time ago, sulkily losing her new-found attraction for Willis to the charms of 4 Stedman Circle . . .

It couldn't be. Still, Celia sweated lightly inside her linen dress, gazed out at the blazing landscape, fished in her bag with an unhurried air for a pair of huge sunglasses which masked her from cheekbones to eyebrows.

People could be so vicious. She did not feel really safe until, after a farewell champagne lunch which America's Deprived Youth would have to fit into the scheme of things somehow, her plane was airborne.

Mrs. Ruykendahl's introductions proved to be as useful as such things generally were. One was, or said she was, coping with a measled child; the other was deep in arrangement for a sister's wedding, after which she and her own husband were departing for a vacation in Bermuda.

Celia, established in a hotel recommended by the consul's widow, was tranquilly pleased at the outcome of her two telephone calls. It had seemed politic to go through the motions, in case she ever wanted some kind of endorsement from LADY, but it was a relief to have severed all connection with the past.

Mrs. Hays-Faulkner could hardly be said to count in this respect. She had obviously been dredged up for a single occasion; moreover, she had said something wistful about returning to the Latin-American country where her husband had served. Celia consulted the notes, bought a map of the city, and studied the newspapers. Not the want ads —there could be nothing of interest to her there—but the society sections.

She had brought with her a certain New York impetus, a kind of confidence that stopped just short of arrogance, and six weeks after her arrival she was being interviewed over tea by two women from the benefit committee of the prestigious Opera Guild. They smiled, assessed, exchanged eye signals like old bridge partners; asked questions like, "Real communication is terribly important, don't you think? And so very hard to achieve."

Celia had learned a good deal of the patter, and when she was at a loss she simply gazed ambiguously into her tea. She knew that she was looking very well-turned-out, even to these Neiman Marcus–oriented eyes: hair wound into a smooth gleam, a single small gold leaf pinned to her ivory suit, bronze gloves cast down as carelessly as though they had not cost her eighteen dollars that morning. She had the air of dallying with the Opera Guild, rather than they with her.

She came shudderingly close to taking the job. Because that evening—the consultation of eyes had decided that perhaps Celia would care to come to one of their little affairs—she met Jules Wain, and he was not a man to have wasted a second look on a woman who worked, in whatever executive capacity.

Although they could not send forth anguished cries from their graves, it was ultimately for Jules Wain that Mr. Tomlinson and Mary Ellen Vestry had died.

Sixteen

A mutual attraction between Jules Wain and Celia was not the wildly unlikely circumstance that it might have seemed.

For her part, Celia recognized that in this man she would come closer to fulfilling all the aims of her life than she had dared to hope. Jules Wain was fifty—but a trim, squash-and-swimming fifty, and in any case the peculiarly youthful charm of Hugh Stevenson, and later David MacIntosh, had long since dissipated. He was a man of considerable wealth and impeccable social position: his wife would find all doors open to her. There were no complicating children from his previous marriage, which had ended several years earlier in divorce. Fairly low on Celia's list came the fact that he was personable enough in an aloof fashion; the pitting of his heavily tanned skin was attractive rather than otherwise.

Wain was equally analytical in his appraisal of the young woman who was introduced to him as Cecelia Brett. The world was full of ravishing females, and his eye was caught less by her undeniable good looks—those shoulders were like something out of a portrait—than her grace of movement and her air of serenity. She was in fact considerably poised for age thirty—Wain misjudged her, approvingly, by three years—and pleasingly single. Perhaps because his former wife was now one, he did not trust divorcees; his mind stamped them quite simply as rejects, cast off because of some fatal flaw. Something euphemistically called temperament, for instance, as in the case of his Brazilian virago.

None but the most surface of these conclusions was arrived at on that first evening, however, and Celia gave no hint of her incredulous exhilaration as she said casually, "I think I met a connection of yours not long ago—Mrs. Hays-Faulkner?"

This was not much of a gamble, in view of the woman's flowered-chiffon propriety, and it turned out to be perfectly safe. Jules Wain's interest in a remote cousin was only deep enough for a courteous lift of the brows and "Oh, Clara's in New York now? How was she?" but it automatically prompted a second look at Celia and, when he and his party left, a smiling inclination of his head toward the table where she sat.

Celia wondered practically how next to proceed. There could be no overt action on her part; all else aside, men like this one would be put off by anything that smacked even faintly of pursuit. Equally, if she took the job with the Opera Guild's benefit committee, she would become little more than a glorified secretary, one of an army of faceless, fashionably dressed women.

One hope lay in the fact that, although Jules Wain had

of course not asked where she was staying, the chances were that she would meet him again in the natural course of events if she played her cards properly. There had been perhaps a hundred people at the Guild's little white-tie affair at the Mark Hopkins, a preponderance of whom had appeared to know each other, and Celia sensed that she had passed more than one kind of screening with honors. It was true that she was an extra woman in a segment of society revolving largely within itself, but she was not a plain or aging or penurious woman—and, thanks to Mrs. Hays-Faulkner, she bore an identifying tag.

Accordingly, she told the sponsors from the Guild that she wasn't actually sure she would settle down in San Francisco—it was so hard to judge a city when you were living in a hotel, wasn't it?—and of course it wouldn't be fair to them to have all the trouble of familiarizing her with the job if she decided not to stay on the Coast after all. Would they possibly know of a nice little place she could rent for a few months? Although she hated to be a bother.

The Guild members, who had once been under the impression that they were weighing and studying Celia, now pursued her with the ardency of greyhounds after a mechanical rabbit. Mrs. Wivenhoe found her a small house on a steeply angled street, with iron-grilled windows and an enclosed back garden with a view of the Bay, and languid Mrs. Phelps aroused herself to suggest a christening party.

The party was given, successfully, ("How *do* you fix those heavenly clams?") and invitations sprang gratifyingly out of it. The Celia who in New York had taken buses instead of taxis, haunted sales, fed herself as frugally as possible, was soon spending a good deal of money on clothes, liquor—it was a social disaster, she had learned, to attempt economy in this area—and imported delicacies; even flowers, occasionally, for the charmingly furnished house on Theodore Street. Although she was as grasping as she had ever been, she watched the money flow away without a pang, because it was not long before the invitations that included her also included Jules Wain.

No duck-hunter had ever built a better blind.

Celia's acceptance into this circle was not greatly to be wondered at. She had after all come to San Francisco with the indirect blessing of Mrs. Hays-Faulkner—and who was to know that the consul's widow had thought she was providing helpful names with a view to a job?—and been presented by Barbara Wivenhoe, who had been a Fitzgerald. She was decorative but not showily so, and the fact that she was not the life of any party was refreshing; her silences were of an enigmatic rather than a tongue-tied nature. She carried with her, more justifiably than any of these people could guess, an aura of personal success and accomplishment, and it was as powerful as the combination to a safe.

None of San Francisco's flavor reached Celia at all. Except as it might affect her own goals, she was peculiarly insensitive to physical atmosphere; it was as though a very shallow vessel had been filled to the brim by one moment of total awareness on a long-ago Christmas Eve at the Vestrys'. She did notice the fogs, because they were a nuisance to her hair, but open water was no novelty to her, the Golden Gate bridge was only a long link between two points, and an overfamiliarity with the preparation of it had bored her with food. All this conveyed an effect of not being easily impressed, and Jules Wain was mildly intrigued by it.

He asked on the first evening when he took her to dinner alone, "Do you find that you miss New York at all?"

Without appearing to, Celia had been studying the restaurant—old, French, apparently famous—and registering in her tireless way that there was evidently a point at which blazing chandeliers and bare marble-topped tables became smarter than low lights and heavy damask. She said with a deliberating air, "Not really. Of course, under the circumstances . . ."

An expression of acute embarrassment quite alien to it appeared on Wain's formidable brown face. "Good Lord, what a stupid question. You look so distracting that I'd forgotten."

Celia gave him a tranquil, understanding smile. Realizing that she would have to produce some reason for arriving on the San Francisco scene, where no friends or relatives awaited her, she had let it be known that a very dear friend of hers, in fact a girl with whom for a time she had shared her New York apartment, had committed suicide, and she had simply wanted to get as far away as possible from painful associations. (Very sensible, said her perspicacious new friends. The best thing to do about such a dreadful experience was to make a clean cut.)

She knew that she was looking extremely well this evening, in polished, scoop-necked ivory satin and the topaz earrings which had become a kind of good-luck charm. The tutelage of Mrs. Pond and Blanca Devlin, plus her own observation, had brought home to her that either stark black or white turned her skin muddy and most blues made it sallow; she was at her best in varying creams

153

or cinnamons or clear deep reds.

But she also knew that a flicker of interested sympathy could settle all too easily into a pall of boredom. She said, lifting her newly arrived daiquiri in answer to Wain's gesture with his Scotch, "I'm afraid I find myself forgetting too. Is that awful of me, or is it just San Francisco?" and he assured her predictably that it did not do to live in the past.

The ordering of dinner, and the careful surveying of it when it arrived, was a protracted and fussy affair in which Celia, far from being amused or annoyed, bathed contentedly. This epitomized what she had striven for: the waiter answering the catechism about the pompano as though the fate of nations were at stake, the precise instructions about the salad dressing. The wine, surprisingly, was presented with smiling confidence and received in kind. Jules Wain was clearly a familiar and valued patron.

They had arrived at coffee when the voice of a woman at the next table struck as sharply at Celia's consciousness as a phrase of English dropped suddenly into a jumble of foreign language. ". . . stepped on a *skateboard*, of all things, but of course being Alec he told everybody he broke it skiing."

There was a little burst of derisive laughter. Celia stared down at her coffee, concentrating fiercely on something at once elusive and beckoning, like the fluttering tag end of a dream. A skateboard, narrowly avoided by her own foot . . . yes, in the narrow dark hall outside the apartment in Bridgeport, although it hadn't been there when she arrived. So a child, or a child plus an older custodian, had come while she was telling that tale to wide-eyed Lena. With terrible faithfulness, Celia's ear now recorded, instead of the restaurant hum, an odd and furtive sound and then Lena's voice saying, "Don't worry, it's only a rat."

Such an urgent warning to secrecy would automatically seem to be worth something in Grand Street, so that *if* someone (someone who had read the address on a Christmas card envelope) had paid an enquiring visit, the child or its companion, possibly hidden that day behind a crack in a peeling door, might very well pursue the visitor out to the street, say slyly, "Were you looking for a lady called Celia? With blonde hair?"

What else had that horribly freshening conversation contained, toward the end? Lena: "Where will you go?" Celia, not meaning it in the least, then, but wanting to put herself an imaginary continent's length away: "California."

It was frightening, even all this safe time later, to realize that she had in effect locked a door and left a window wide open. Celia moved her shoulders in a quick tense shudder, and Jules Wain said solicitously, "Chilly?" She shook her head, smiling, secure again, and leaned forward conspiratorially. "Someone has a friend who stepped on a skateboard. Doesn't that sound painful?"

She went to bed that night with a pleasure that bordered cautiously on triumph. She congratulated herself on her intuitive feeling that Jules Wain was basically very conventional and had been reassured rather than otherwise when he was not asked in for a drink at close to midnight. He had held her one hand in both of his, lightly but possessively, as he said, "I'm leaving for New York Sunday night. I'll be gone two weeks, so I'd like to call you before then if I may."

"Please do," said Celia with warmth but no alarming

eagerness. She knew that the background of the foyer became her so well that it gave the impression of having been done in detail by her own hand, and that the faint appreciative tip of Wain's head as he said good night was measuring her in other and more familiar doorways.

His trip to New York aroused no flicker of apprehension. He had made it clear that his interest in Celia was more than casual, but even if he were the kind of man to look into past history before committing himself—and Celia suspected coolly that he was—what could he discover? She had kept her life tightly compartmented, so that if he took the trouble to look up his distant cousin, in whom he had shown only the most perfunctory interest, he could still only be led back as far as Blanca Devlin and LADY. Blanca did not even suspect the existence of Mrs. Pond and the Hotel Alexandra; Mrs. Pond, in turn, knew nothing of the Vestrys or Mr. Tomlinson.

So Celia retired contentedly in her elegant little shell on Theodore Street. Her own particular brand of cruelty had no conception—then—of the remorseless patience with which a watcher could allow a beetle to toil up a slippery surface and let it reach the very lip before flicking it contemptuously to the bottom.

She had wronged Jules Wain in her appraisal. In that respect, she was even safer than she knew.

Like many successful men, Wain had a boundless respect for his own judgment of people. He knew, and vaguely approved the fact, that the corporation of which he was board chairman took long hard looks at would-be file clerks and, when it came to secretaries, dug into references like a terrier after rats. Well and good; that was the function of personnel departments. To suggest that Jules Wain himself go in search of supportive evidence in the case of a young woman who attracted him strongly would be to imply an intolerable slur on his powers of assessment. He would feel like a yokel furtively trying to scratch glass with a sparkling stone.

It was true that his first marriage had been a disaster from which his memory flinched even now, but just as ships' hulls had been restructured after the Titanic, so had his views of women. He had acquired a protective shield against vivacity and dazzle, and he did not care at all for cocktail wit, which he somehow lumped in with divorcees. Widows, simply because they had outlived their husbands and this carried a lurking unpleasantness for a man who took good physical care of himself, had no appeal.

But Celia Brett, now—obviously good family; no trouble there. Attractive, clearly healthy, and . . . thoughtful. Poised. Even-tempered; not one of the ecstasy-or-despair females who lit up an evening like a rocket and could be found fizzling in a hangover the next day. When he had been in New York a week, Wain telephoned Celia. The following morning he sent her flowers.

Celia brightened the interval before his return in learning what she could about the divorce. She was growing increasingly confident, and it would be helpful to know where your predecessor had gone wrong—because as Jules had money and social position, there could be no other side of it.

She said carelessly to Barbara Wivenhoe, "It's nice to meet a man who doesn't go around casting the blame on his ex-wife, at least."

157

"Well, Jules doesn't actually have to, if it comes to that. I never knew her—they were living in Chicago then —but we had friends who did, and it seems that she was given to making the most appalling public scenes. Which of course wasn't doing Jules the least little bit of good with his company," said Mrs. Wivenhoe with critical detachment. "The polite version was that she had had a nervous breakdown, but everybody could see that the real trouble was drinking. So . . ."

Celia was not chilled at the cool expediency of such a divorce, but relieved. Something neutral like "incompatibility" would have given her no guideline at all.

The weeks after Jules's return from New York were for Celia like walking a tightrope with no slack at all. To take even more pains with her appearance than before, to be available when he called without an air of hanging hopefully about the telephone, to pretend pleasure at events like a horse show and a performance of Gilbert and Sullivan—to do all this and still maintain her attitude of relaxed poise was a severe strain. She knew that it was going to be worthwhile on an evening when Wain, having kissed her with more than his usual warmth, asked her to lunch at his home the next day to meet the widowed sister-in-law who acted as his hostess.

Up until now, in what was a considered approach rather than a courtship, they had moved on neutral and uncommitted ground, in the company of an age group younger than Wain's, older than Celia's, which assimilated them both with ease. Celia knew of the existence of Adelaide Corliss Wain, and at once sensed an enemy in the person of an older woman so comfortably entrenched. Accordingly, she dressed and readied herself the next day with
158

the care used so infinitely long ago in preparing to meet a strange girl who had an apartment to share.

Even aside from the fact that he owned it, as a convenient way of life for a bachelor who was absent from his domain a good deal of the time, Wain's apartment had the spacious and settled air of a luxurious home. A uniformed maid opened the door, and Celia, piloted lightly by Jules's hand under her arm, had a confused impression of heavy rugs, the quiet gleam of mirrors, paneling set here and there with lighted paintings, and ultimately Mrs. Wain, ensconced in a pale-blue brocade chair.

Mrs. Wain, a fragile, handsome, gray-haired woman a few years older than her brother-in-law, smiled through introductions, apologized charmingly for her infirmity—arthritis—and revealed herself as the opposition when the maid came to stand expectantly in the doorway. "Do you care to take something before lunch, Miss Brett?" (Another drinker in the house.) "We have some really excellent sherry—"

Jules turned his face impassively to the maid. "Miss Brett will have a daiquiri, I'll have Scotch on the rocks. Adelaide . . . ?"

"Having recommended the sherry, I shall have to have it, shan't I?" inquired Mrs. Wain humorously. But she was unvanquished; wearing a hostess smile as implacably as a conventioneer's lapel button, she proceeded to put Celia through her paces.

"Jules tells me you're from Connecticut originally, so we're both New Englanders. I was brought up in Boston. I have some very dear friends in Wilton, do you know that area at all?"

"Only vaguely, I'm afraid, but it's very pretty as I remember it from drives. We lived outside Danbury," said Celia, smiling back.

"The hat place, of course," said Mrs. Wain with a musing air. "Such beautiful country around about, though— but so changed, as I imagine much of the East is nowadays. Have you been back recently?"

"Since my mother's death three years ago, no."

"Celia's been in New York," said Jules with undisguised sharpness. "I told you, that's where she met Clara Hays-Faulkner."

"Of course, I'd forgotten. How *is* Clara? Did you look her up while you were in New York this time, Jules?"

"I did think of it, but she isn't in the book." Jules glanced at his watch. "Didn't David—my secretary," he said offside to Celia, "say he'd be here by one fifteen?"

"He did, but he's obviously been delayed. I'm sure Miss Brett would like another cocktail," said Mrs. Wain, delicately venomous, "so we can put the time to good—Oh, there you are, David."

A shadow had fallen over the beautiful rug. Celia, in the act of shaking her head and refusing another cocktail, glanced up at the man walking through the doorway and set her glass down blindly in the space an inch from the table's edge.

Seventeen

The tall fair man who had entered was not David Mac-
Intosh—could not have been, Celia realized later, outside of some computer-arranged nightmare—but the set
of his head and shoulders against the light, his Christian
name, the inimical Mrs. Wain's air of satisfaction at his
arrival, had all conspired to do the damage. The stemmed
glass struck the rug soundlessly, letting out a tiny darkening gulp of liquid on the Persian flowers; Mrs. Wain's
astonished gaze traced a triangle from Celia to the secretary to Jules and back again. Celia put a hand to her forehead as though to press back dizziness. "I'm so sorry—"

Sorry didn't begin to cover it: she had seen the look of
faintly distasteful surprise, as if he were watching a
clumsy stranger, that crossed Jules's face before concern
took over. While Mrs. Wain assured her smoothly that it
didn't matter in the least, that table was *much* too small,
and insisted on providing a fresh cocktail, Celia's mind began to race.

David Farrell joined them for lunch in the small formal

dining room. Although it was evident from his manner that this was not the first time he had done so, he was still somewhat discomfited by the reaction to his entrance and glanced covertly at Celia from time to time. This was not lost on Mrs. Wain; Celia, now recovered, noted with cold amusement that as soup gave way to mushroom omelette and tiny fresh peas, to be replaced in turn by strawberries and coffee, the older woman grew almost benevolent. The triumphant shape of what she planned to say later to Jules —"Mark my words, there's something between those two, or there has been"—hovered almost as tangibly as the white-coated manservant.

Let her dig herself deeper: although Farrell left immediately after coffee, Celia did not mention him until she and Jules had arrived back at Theodore Street. There, in the lemon-and-white foyer, she asked with an air of uncharacteristic hesitation, "You can stay a few minutes, can't you, Jules? And would you get us a brandy? It's silly of me, but I still feel a little shaken up . . . It was Mr. Farrell," she said, taking the liqueur glass he handed her and giving a shiver which was only half-assumed. "I thought when he came in that he was the man who drove the girl I've told you about to suicide—there's an uncanny resemblance, and his name was David too—and it brought the whole thing back so dreadfully . . ."

She knew as she talked, watching Jules, that an explanation had been essential and this particular explanation wise; a certain thoughtfulness in his regard was being replaced by solicitude and, if she wasn't mistaken, a masculine pleasure at what he took to be her tenderer sensibilities. Moreover she was, in a sense, speaking with sincerity. The momentary assumption that she was looking at David

MacIntosh had been terrifying, like a loose thread, free for the seizing, which could unravel all her work and expose the discarded past.

And, like most things, it had two edges. Sharp reaction of any kind generated a counter-reaction, created a tiny unwilling bond. The secretary, saying good-bye to Celia, had given her an acutely personal look which she hadn't liked at all.

"Poor darling, I can see how it would have upset you," said Jules, tightening his arm protectively about her. "Farrell isn't the villain, you know, he's worked for me since—well, years, anyway, and I doubt that he has time to do much philandering here, let alone in New York. Still—" he was perturbed, only half-joking "we may have to have him grow a mustache. I don't believe I could tolerate a beard."

Celia's heart leaped at the implication that she would be seeing a fair amount of any secretary of Jules's as a matter of course; it was far more committing than any embrace. She released herself gently and, remembering Adelaide Wain's anticipatory relish, smiled. "Would you explain to your sister-in-law? I don't know what she can have thought of me."

A week later, Jules asked Celia to marry him.

It was a considered proposal rather than an impetuous one, the orderly progress to a goal marked out beforehand, and Celia was too wise to pretend to any happy confusion. Confusion was not a state which appealed to Jules Wain: he had been heard to remark that equanimity was a hallmark of breeding. Celia accepted him with a radiant calm which gave no hint of her wild elation; it would have seemed ridiculous to compare her to a runner breasting the tape. She did catch her breath when she saw the ring—not with involuntary pleasure, as Jules assumed, but out of a sense of triumph that attacked almost as sharply as pain.

And she was glad that she had gotten at least some of the details of the divorce from Barbara Wivenhoe. This way, although there was a kind of silent warning in the air that the subject of Jules's first wife should never be brought up, Celia was prepared for his blunt dislike of the press and his suggestion that they keep the announcement brief: his company's public relations department would release it if Celia had no objection.

Accordingly, under the poised, not-quite-smiling portrait she had taken at Jules's request, she was identified in the society section as Cecelia Louise Brett—she gave herself Louise as a bonus, having always thought it a name of immense gentility—formerly of New York City; daughter of the late Mr. and Mrs. James M. Brett. She was reading the clipping for perhaps the twentieth time ("Mr. Wain is board chairman of Cyprex, Inc., wood-products corporation") when a memory came bobbing to the surface with the unexpectedness of a corpse released from the sea floor.

The Vestrys had a married son out on the coast: at some point in time David MacIntosh had told her that. A doctor, a lawyer, something like that. But the coast contained any number of locations for professional men—San Diego, Los Angeles . . . Starting the list comfortingly for herself, Celia threw in the reassuring reminder that lots of people, maybe most people, never glanced at the society page of a newspaper at all.

By this time she had ruffled to the V's in the telephone

164

directory, and there it was: Vestry, Paul H. Jr., veterinary surgeon.

But it was over two years since Mary Ellen had taken her own life, with her own sleeping pills, and no matter what wild tale Susan Vestry had told her brother at the time Celia's name had, in all probability, faded out of his mind long ago. Besides, was it likely that a veterinarian would so much as pause at the wedding and engagement announcements? And if by chance his wife's eye had fallen upon "Cecelia Brett to Wed Socialite Jules Wain," she would be even less apt than Paul Vestry to make any connection. It was foolish to have such a very clear vision of one saying, "You don't suppose this could be *the* Celia Brett . . . ? She does come from New York," and the other replying, "Why don't you tear it out and send it to Susan?"

Celia had not arrived at her present position in life by any blind optimism. She did not delude herself into thinking that time had softened Susan to the point where, seeing Celia on the brink of an eminently advantageous marriage, she would simply shrug and forget about it. Not with that face of almost incandescent grief and anger . . .

Perhaps because her waking moments were so tirelessly absorbed in the preserving of her own image and the furthering of her ambitions, Celia almost never dreamed; it was as though some kindly psychical nurse took over and said, "You need your strength for tomorrow." But she dreamed that night, if a flashing jumble of scenes could be called dreaming. What frightened her most was the face of the Vestrys' housekeeper, turned sharp and vindictive as the woman pushed an apron at her and said in a deep harsh voice, "Peel those beans, I told you! They're waiting for their dinner in there!"

How to peel beans . . . ? Celia woke, and the dreaded apron was a tangle of sheet, the hardness biting into her right palm her ring and not a paring knife's handle. But the fear lingered; even after tomato juice and coffee, which was all the breakfast she allowed herself, it was hard to shake off the feeling that something unpleasant and mocking had taken place while she slept.

She restrained herself from calling Jules at his office to examine his voice for any possible change of mood; he would regard such a call as irksomely girlish, and in any case they were meeting for lunch. Have to get things organized before their wedding trip abroad, he had told her smilingly; he didn't think Cyprex would fall to pieces in six months without him but he'd be spending a good deal of time in rescheduled meetings.

Celia was astonished at the ease with which a wedding could be planned at the Wain level. Adelaide Wain, bowing to the inevitable and assuming an air of sweetness as false as a borrowed mustache—"As you haven't your dear mother, perhaps you'd allow me to help"—wrote down dates and made lists and appointments with the aid of Jules's secretary, a sandy middle-aged woman who had quietly replaced David Farrell. It was agreed that the guest list should be small, so as not to emphasize the total lack of family or family friends on Celia's side (anticipating questions, she pretended to write to and receive heartfelt regrets from a few people in the East) but wealth automatically wiped out the usual bother of decisions.

Such as where they would live on their return from Europe. During their absence Jules's sister-in-law would oversee the complete redecoration of the master bedroom and then erase herself from the apartment, leaving it as a comfortable base from which they could look over suitable properties at their leisure. It was the redecorating as much as the magnificent diamond that had borne in upon Celia the extent of her success. The New York apartment had been furnished expensively and with taste, and the Theodore Street house had a stage-set perfection, but both backgrounds were ready-made. Although Celia was not consciously stamped with the memory of maids' rooms, the taste of victory had never been sweeter than when swatches and paint samples and furniture designs were submitted for her approval, with no niggling considerations as to cost.

The years of poring over the magazines devoted to the great of her world ("Mrs. Thomas Benton Knowles II chooses jade and white for her charming sitting room at Broadmere, the Knowles' summer home at Newport") paid off handsomely. Even in the grudging eyes of Adelaide Wain, Celia did not put a foot wrong.

Could all this now be in the balance?

In the restaurant where she had arrived first, Celia watched Jules presently threading his way toward her, urbane, well-tailored, lifting a hand occasionally in greeting. He paused once at a table where a white-haired general stood up to shake his hand cordially; after a moment both men turned to gaze across the intervening tables at Celia, who tipped her head a little and smiled in recognition of the general's gallant bow. She knew that Jules enjoyed presenting her to people, even at a distance, and it did not distress her in the least that at such times he took on their air of interested but uninvolved appraisal, much like a man joining in the inspection of a costly new car.

As usual when Jules was seated, there was a waiter there at once. Also as usual, Jules offered a cocktail punctiliously although he himself almost never drank at lunch, a discipline in accord with his twice-weekly twenty laps in his club's pool, but here there was a departure from custom. Instead of declining, Celia said with promptness, "I'd love one."

Jules regarded her with faint apprehension. He knew that she was to have spent a part of the morning at the apartment with Adelaide, deciding which china and silver should be kept and which sent to storage. He also knew that his sister-in-law's frosty dislike of Celia was as strong as ever under her benevolent smiles, and like any other man he had hoped that a truce could be maintained until the wedding. If, on the other hand, Adelaide was going to start ruffling his pleasant world—

Celia read his expression accurately. "No, darling, nothing like that. I didn't get to the apartment at all; in fact, I seem to have spent the entire morning on the phone. The Friths want to give us an enormous cocktail party next week, and someone on the Examiner society staff asked about our wedding trip, and a photographer will do the pictures for nothing if we let him do some exclusive shots of us both in various spots in your apartment."

She gazed at him with delicate ruefulness over the rim of the daiquiri she hadn't wanted at all and had only ordered to guarantee a little extra alertness on Jules's part. "It's impossible, I know, but I had the maddest wish that we could just go off and be married quietly somewhere where we don't know a soul."

This was a carefully three-pronged attack. It strengthened the illusion that Celia was not marrying Jules for the

168

sake of wealth and parade; it catered to his own distaste for publicity; it posed a challenge. Unless she were very much mistaken, he would say—

Jules considered olives, decided against them, helped himself to a spoonful of marinated mushrooms. He said with deliberation, "Why is it impossible?"

Celia dropped her lashes to conceal her cautious jubilation. "Oh, Jules. Your sister-in-law"—she refused to say Mrs. Wain and could not quite venture upon Adelaide—"has been to so much trouble. The invitations haven't gone to the engraver yet, but all your friends . . . people will expect . . ."

She could not have hit on a more successful note. Jules Wain's innate arrogance seldom came to the surface—seldom had to—but it was there immediately in the measured lift of his still-dark brows. "'People?' Politicians have to defer to them, of course, but our marriage is hardly in the public domain." He had liked the mushrooms; he took more, with an air of growing absorption. "Odd how these coincidences come up. I was on the phone this morning with a friend of mine who owns a lodge in Santa Fe. He's a great ski-country enthusiast, naturally, and he suggested that we have the wedding there."

"Oh? Do you know, I've always wanted to see Santa Fe," said Celia, sounding only dreamily reflective. She stroked the stem of her glass with a steady finger, as though she did not feel her safety to be balanced on a knife edge.

"It's quite—distinctive," said Jules temperately as the waiter placed deviled crab before them, "and surprisingly cosmopolitan. According to Roger, the mountain view from his lodge—he's called it The Priory—is spectacular

169

at this time of year."

The small salt-and-pepper busying interval was less like a silence than a tapestry beginning to show a few colored threads.

"Of course, it would be extremely cold, but it's a dry cold because of the altitude," said Jules.

"That's what I've heard," said Celia, still carefully idle; she had heard nothing of the kind, and was not even entirely sure what state Santa Fe was in. Colorado? New Mexico? Fairly far removed from San Francisco, at any rate.

Jules gave the crab his judicious attention—he was not a man to whom meals made only a necessary division of the day—but Celia's idea was clearly gaining ground. He squeezed lemon with an air of thought. "There'd be a minimum residency period, but I shouldn't imagine it would be more than three days or so. I'll have Mrs. Dewey look into it this afternoon."

Careful . . . careful. "Darling, do you think we actually could? Just have it tiny and quiet and anonymous, with no newspaper fuss?"

A wistfulness in Celia's tone, a lingering suggestion that there might be something which even Jules Wain could not acceptably do, was perhaps the strongest card of all. "If it's what we want," said Jules, slipping automatically into the plural, "I don't know who's to stop us."

Anyone watching them might have been reminded of a pair of children, about to take possession of a tree house—of hand-crafted mahogany, furnished by Sloan. Celia gave Jules a glowing look. "Let's not tell *anybody*," she said.

But of course it was not quite as simple at that. Adelaide Wain and a few of Jules's close friends had to be told, and party-givers like the Friths, who had counted upon being included in a pleasant round of other prewedding parties, advised vaguely that the principals had not yet set a firm date.

For Christmas, Celia gave Jules gold cufflinks, and received a slender, supple rivulet of diamonds and emeralds for her wrist. Adelaide Wain's present proved to be the thinnest of white cashmere shawls, for which Celia could imagine no use whatever; she tendered Jules's sister-in-law another figurine to add to the Dresden collection which would shortly have to be moved to new quarters, and was rewarded with a smile of enormous frost. "How thoughtful of you, dear. I've always been afraid that something would happen to the milkmaid—even the best of hotel maids can be careless—and it's so nice to have two."

On the day after New Year's they were in Santa Fe. During the mandatory three-day wait after the license, Jules stayed at The Priory, a dauntingly exclusive lodge north of the city, as did Adelaide Wain, who had seemed genuinely horrified that the wedding could be contemplated without a family representative. Celia was chastely installed at an elegant old hotel only a block or two from Santa Fe's plaza. She was vaguely frightened of the blanketed Indians with their wares, and although she said, "Yes, aren't they?" when it was pointed out to her with great frequency that the Sangre de Cristo mountains were magnificent, she found them a monumental bore.

But the time passed pleasantly enough. Most of the people looked either sleek and expensive or wildly disheveled and artistic, and the Celia whose years-ago ambition it had been to have heads turn as she passed, and voices murmur, "That's Celia Brett," was delighted that she attracted no more than the automatic glances accorded tall blonde young women everywhere.

She was relatively unworried about what might happen *after* she became Mrs. Jules Wain. It was true that Jules had divorced one wife, but that was for a socially acceptable reason. His pride would never allow him to appear to have been tricked, particularly if Celia returned from Europe pregnant, as she was coldly determined to do. The six months abroad would provide that much indemnity, and she did not look beyond.

In the meantime, she was blessedly anonymous and safe from nagging little worries like the insurance-company convention she had seen announced in the lobby of a San Francisco hotel just before they left, and the abruptly remembered existence of Mary Ellen Vestry's older brother. (Surely a big rangy woman like Mrs. Vestry *had* recovered from her collapse?)

Here in Santa Fe, no one knew of the old Celia . . .

Or so she had thought until tonight.

Eighteen

A faint smell of smoke, the essence of all danger signals, still hung in the hotel room from the burning of the note. It was not quite six thirty, but how much time was she to be allowed? Enough, obviously, to encompass her own destruction. If her facial muscles had not been so rigid with purpose, Celia could almost have smiled at that.

There was no point now in trying to sift faces on the plane or at the airport; she need not have been followed at all. Although Jules had agreed indulgently to keep the place and time of their wedding as secret as was practicable, the simplest of ruses could have obtained it from his secretary; it wasn't a matter of industrial security. While Celia had strolled unworriedly about the shops that bordered the plaza, or waited for Jules in the hotel lobby, she had very probably been under observation by the enemy, already established in Santa Fe and delaying the attack until the last minute so as to give it maximum effectiveness.

Established where? At The Priory, almost certainly. It

was implicit in the note that the writer would *know* whether or not the wedding had been canceled, and where else but at the proposed scene could the knowledge be had so quickly? Even a brief acquaintance with the inner life of hotels had taught Celia that nothing sped as rapidly among the staff, or caused such giggling speculation, as the eleventh-hour calling off of a wedding. The signs would be there for an eye trained for them—and if they were not, there would be the threatened personal approach to Jules, although that meant giving up the extra twist of the knife.

Celia had of course considered and discarded the two obvious possibilities. She could telephone Jules at once— it was a blessing that he was a traditionalist and had taken it for granted that he would not be seeing her the evening before the wedding—and say that she had just had an anonymous and frightening telephone call, and could they be married right away, tonight, by a justice of the peace?

But Jules Wain was not an impetuous, infatuated boy. He would be concerned and outraged, and want the police informed, and interrogate the switchboard operators and learn that no call had been put through to Room 218 within the last several hours .Long before any of this transpired, Adelaide Wain would have remarked triumphantly that there was something very peculiar here, to say the least, and how much did Jules actually *know* about his fiancée?

Or Celia could feign illness—even, if necessary, do herself a minor injury and insist that Jules and Adelaide return to San Francisco without her. But that would only postpone disaster; "this wedding" did not mean simply "this ceremony." Celia was sure to her bones that if she did not marry Jules at The Priory in the morning she would never get to marry him at all. She was equally sure that, her capital badly depleted and the only part of San Francisco that mattered closed to her ("She was engaged to Jules Wain, but there must have been some really grisly skeleton in the cupboard because it was called off at the last minute") such a chance would never come her way again.

Celia had not thrust old Mr. Tomlinson over the balcony all those years ago, nor had she force-fed Mary Ellen Vestry an overdose of sleeping pills. But the pattern that allowed destruction was there, as distinct in her nature as her blood type. It enabled her to face with calm the fact that in the course of the next few fours she would have to flush out, and permanently dispose of, her patient enemy.

First things first. Celia's hand had drawn back from the telephone a few minutes earlier; now she picked up the receiver and gave the operator The Priory number. Her emerald-cut diamond, badge of everything she had worked and schemed and waited for, glistened coldly up at her.

"Hi, darling," she said in a relaxed and sleepy voice when Jules answered. "I just called to say that the altitude is catching up with me or something, and if I don't want to be a haggard bride I think I'd better soak a while and then have a sandwich sent up and crawl into bed. I might even take a seconal."

"Good idea," said Jules over five miles of wintry New Mexico darkness. "It *is* only that? You don't feel ill?"

"Not a bit—just that I could use a little extra sleep," said Celia through a daintily audible yawn. "We did get in quite a lot of sightseeing today, you know."

And they had, driving in the rented car to a pueblo

south of Santa Fe, walking about the trading post there—on top of that, traipsing through the museum in the Palace of the Governors, where Celia had had to exclaim over a number of dreadful old bowls.

"I know what you mean, I'm feeling it a bit myself and I think I'll have a tray here too," said Jules, and they exchanged fond but brisk good nights. And that was that: Celia was assured of no calls from The Priory to an unanswering telephone here. She crossed the room to her suitcase, tipped up the lid, and rummaged in a side pocket for the weapon, if it could be called that, which she had packed at the last minute only because Jules had bought it for her and he might inquire.

Six weeks earlier, in a house on Theodore Street only three removed from Celia's, the housekeeper in charge while the owners were vacationing in the Bahamas had been attacked by a young hoodlum whose apparent motive was violence: he had beaten her senseless, smashed some furniture, and left without touching any of the inviting silver in evidence. When apprehended, he was under the influence of drugs.

Jules was not only alarmed on Celia's behalf but outraged at this departure from the rules; like most sensible and well-insured men, his credo was to turn over any valuables without demur rather than risk being knifed or shot. But there were obviously cases where this did not apply, particularly among women living alone, and he had insisted on providing Celia with a plastic tear-gas gun which, shot at close range, would immobilize an intruder for the time necessary to an escape.

Open air would lessen the effect of the gas but there would still be seconds, at least, when the advantage was Celia's.

It was thanks to her unusual fringe attention, developed over the years, that she had remembered without a small item in the local newspaper, read on the day after her arrival in Santa Fe. The body of an elderly man had been fished out of the shallow, iced-over alameda which emerged from its underground course in this part of the city. The autopsy report indicated that he had been stunned by either a fall or a blow—there was alcohol involved and the evidence wasn't conclusive—and had died of exposure in the bitter temperature.

Death by exposure was a natural process, Celia now reasoned to herself, and overtook the young and healthy as well as the old; lost hikers were prone to it, for example, and mountain climbers. It wasn't really murder, it was the extension of an accident. And how would the police make a connection between an accident victim, carefully anonymous behind an unsigned note deposited at a hotel desk, and Mrs Jules Wain, abroad on her honeymoon?

For that matter, identification alone would take time in the case of a visitor to the city if there were no handbag, or no wallet.

Celia dropped the gas gun into her own handbag, consulted the menu on the desk, called room service and ordered a meal which she had no intention of eating beyond a few hunger-allaying bites. From her suitcase she took the navy ski-suit she had bought because, like all sports clothes, it became her—and, tonight, would melt easily into darkness. She carried the suit and a sweater into the bedroom, along with a pair of soft warm boots and a scarf which was red on one side and emerald on the other, and returned to the bedroom for the most concentrated thought of her life. The room-service waiter to whom she presently called "Come in" found her sitting relaxedly in the room's one armchair, apparently engrossed in a thick paperback edition of *War and Peace* bought in Jules's company in the lobby. ("I haven't read this in *ages.*")

She said idly as she tipped the waiter, "I imagine it's getting quite cold out?" and gave an appreciative little shiver, the reaction of a woman settled comfortably in for the night, when he answered politely that the temperature was expected to drop to twelve.

Her face was already made up. She changed rapidly into the ski-suit and boots, consuming during the process a slice of chicken and a half a buttered roll, simply as fodder. At the last minute she took an envelope from the desk—it was marked distinctively with the hotel's name, but you saw them all over Santa Fe—addressed it randomly to Mrs. Howard Wright, The Priory, scrawled a few words on a sheet of paper, inserted it. In the bathroom, whose tile floor seemed always to hold an invisible film of moisture, she stepped on the envelope, picked it up and put it carefully in her bag.

She met no one on the stairs, and at the side exit she chose there were only a few strange women tourists peering hungrily into the window of a closed and lighted shop. Not much over an hour after she had received the ultimatum, Celia was across the plaza, carefully avoiding the taxi rank at the hotel front, and in a cab on her way to The Priory.

In defiance of local tradition, the lodge was built not of adobe but of imported gray stone, unexpected and coolly soothing to the eye. By daylight, with colored pennons streaming from its heights against a background of piñon-clad foothills, it had an air at once cloistered and battle-mented. By night, austerely eschewing any neon or other notice beyond a chaste and floodlit one at the foot of its upwinding drive, it was a collection of soft warm gold among folds of icy darkness. The most inexperienced of tourists, unless he had a very well-padded wallet, would have driven by the wrought-iron gates in search of the more familiar scarlet and green and blue twinkles prepared for any travelers at all.

When Celia's cab deposited her at the huge, semicircu-lar forecourt, she said fretfully to the driver as she paid him, "My luggage was sent on ahead from Colorado, and I do hope it's here," but that was the only compromise she made with Fate. A reluctant gambler who had been forced to a single throw, she mounted shallow stone steps and entered The Priory.

In her hotel room, the telephone which had begun to ring before she reached the street commenced again. From its discreetly muted warbling there might have been no urgency at all, no life hanging in the balance.

Nineteen

The warmth of the lobby was almost dizzying after the penetrating cold outside, and although the lighting was as subdued as that of a private living room it was not a remarkable gesture for Celia to let her upswung dark glasses drop casually into place. She had been to The Priory on the morning of their arrival in Santa Fe, to inspect the small formal room in which the marriage ceremony would take place, but she stood for seconds just inside the heavy carved doors as though getting her bearings. With most of her pale hair concealed by the emerald side of the head scarf, she would be to all observers but one just another woman in well-cut ski clothes.

Oriental rugs on flagstone floors, islanded chairs and sofas, a pair of black Great Danes coming unhurriedly to their haunches before the flaming logs in a huge fireplace: at this hour there were only five people not occupied elsewhere with drinks or dinner. Celia wondered flashingly if the slender haunted-looking woman in gray tweed could be Susan Vestry—she was the kind who would have grown leaner rather than plump with the years—or the turning-away profile of a woman with a fall of very black hair concealed the yellow stare of Mrs. Cannon, or the heavy-set man all abulge with muscles and handknit red and green reindeer housed the old Willis Lambert. (It was the kind of thing Willis would wear.)

The other two people were an elegant old lady of perhaps eighty and a questionable one: a person who either hadn't seen his barber in some time or liked her medium-colored hair very short. This one wore round tinted glasses which dazzled briefly at Celia and tipped downward again. And that was all—

No, it wasn't. From over the back of the wing chair which had been slightly turned away from its intended grouping rose a wavering stream of cigarette smoke.

Celia walked to the desk at her right, with the conviction that she had pulled one gaze after her like a slipstream. She didn't turn, because it was essential at this point to give the impression of being convinced that she had shaken off her enemy for the time being and was safe here. She took from her bag the envelope she had prepared in her room, and leaned forward a little to address the desk clerk in a low and confidential tone.

What she said was, "I found this outside in your court-yard just now. It isn't stamped, so I imagine someone will be calling for it," and what the clerk replied after a glance at the writing was, "Thank you very much. One of our guests must have dropped it," but from a distance the interchange had a secret-keeping air. The clerk turned to the ranked boxes behind him and stowed the envelope under W.

W for the figmentary Mrs. Howard Wright, of course,

but surely, to a single-minded observer, W for Wain?

It was inevitably more difficult for Celia than for most people to put herself in another's place, but to her—as Jules Wain had not left The Priory, nor caused his and his sister-in-law's luggage to be furiously assembled in the lobby—this would have the air of a plan. If it had been Celia's intention to submit to the ultimatum so meekly, wouldn't it have been more logical to send a messenger with the letter on this bitterly cold night, while she herself stayed at her hotel and arranged for departure the next day?

Instead of which she was here at The Priory, had just murmured to the desk clerk, was now pushing back the cuff of her jacket and checking her wrist watch with the huge modernistic clock high on the wall. It was a gesture common in public places, and would have possible significance to only one watcher. In a matter of moments, now, she would know whether this desperate gamble was paying off and she was actually being followed.

The fury which had possessed her earlier was gone. She was as utterly, queerly calm as the day when she had stood in an old-fashioned bedroom at Stedman Circle and watched—

With decision but no hurry, a woman who had made up her mind to go on into the cocktail lounge and secure a table while she waited for her companion, Celia passed the desk and turned to her right in the direction of the corridor with the soft gold sign that said "The Wreath Room." There was also a powder room along the way, and public telephone booths, and a mirrored little alcove and, at the far end of the corridor, an exit onto one of the terraces that ran along the back of the lodge.

The propped-wide glass door of the cocktail lounge, as she passed it, gave Celia what was in effect an around-the-corner reflection of a portion of the lobby. The woman in gray tweed was no longer there, and the wing chair was empty. In an ashtray on the table beside it, a cigarette which had been only partially extinguished out of carelessness or haste was sending up a furred column of smoke.

Celia did not dare turn her head. She gave a quick little wave at the untenanted terrace in its fringe of darkness and slipped rapidly through the door.

The iron purpose that had left no room for rage was also a shield against the cold, deepened by a wind that Celia hadn't noticed in the taxi or the protected forecourt. If anything she felt the icy brush of it reassuring, an ally against whoever it was who had just emerged from The Priory behind her, making a pulse of paler gold on the flagstones like someone breathing on a flame. The woman in gray? The occupant of the wing chair?

On her brief visit here three days earlier, with Adelaide addressing the manager firmly about the wedding arrangements, Celia had stood at a window and noted without any particular interest a small artificial pond, sunken and iron-railed, behind a wing of the lodge. She had thought idly at the time that as it was obviously too small for skating it must have some decorative display in the summer—goldfish, or birds, or lilies. At present, and especially so in her mind's eye for the last hour, it was a frozen lightless gray under blown veils of snow, no more hospitable than concrete to someone crashing heavily down onto it.

Celia turned left in the almost total blackness of the night, guided by the pale stiff ruffle of snow left from the clearing of the brick path. And in the distance behind her, in a voice half blown away by the wind, someone called her name.

Celia's heart gave a great pound of triumph, because although she had imagined that she heard or felt a faint impact of following feet along the path, and even a click that might have been a woman's high heel coming incautiously down, there was always the possibility that the pursuer had suddenly sensed danger, and realized that the pretense of flight was a deadly ploy with certain animals. She did not halt or even slow beyond the necessary few seconds to fumble the gas gun out of her bag, because the trap was now only yards away: the rigid bars of the railing around the lake, and the pale curls of frozen snow in the staggery shape that was a piñon tree at one side of the stone steps down. She reached the tree and crouched beside it, gloved finger on the plastic trigger.

Oddly, in view of her purpose here, she had no fear for her own physical safety. *She* wasn't intended to die but to live and see her success mocked and the prize snatched away at the last minute. Celia knew, she supposed she had always known, that there was only one person capable of this calm, dry-eyed remorselessness.

. . . And here she came, scarfed like Celia, looking taller and somehow bulkier from this perspective, swinging the round darkness of her head from side to side in a baffled way. Celia had taken off the glove after all, because the gun was a household defense and not designed to accommodate wool, and now, springing to her feet, she pulled the trigger, grasped a staggering shoulder, caught the other, and pushed with all her strength.

There had been a deep convulsive sound of anger and alarm when the gun went off with a surprisingly crisp crack, but after that there was only a single thump as the figure hit the stone stairs once and then a hollow echoing knock as it struck the ice. The ice held, but Celia, filtering out her own harsh breathing, thought that there must be water underneath; nothing else could produce that drumming effect. She moved to the top of the steps, wiping her eyes although the wind had been with her and she had received only a whiff of the gas, and stared down.

Susan Vestry did not stir. She had evidently somersaulted when she struck a stair-edge because she lay almost on her back, a surprisingly big-looking, dead-looking crumple of black on the vaguely paler ice. But almost certainly not dead, thought Celia; people survived astonishing falls all the time. Was she unconscious enough, damaged enough for the penetrating cold to do the rest?

Better make sure. Another rap against the ice . . . and in any case Celia had to retrieve the gun, which had left her hand as she pushed. It would hardly contribute to the theory of accident, and although she had never been fingerprinted and there was no surface connection between her and Susan Vestry, she would feel better with it back.

She started down the steps, already busy with the problem of getting back to her hotel, pushing away two little horrors that were beginning to thrust at her like glass slivers. These were *booted* feet—she was close enough to see that now—so where had the heel-click on the path come from? (A tree branch, cracking in the cold.) Women surprised by attack usually screamed, or squealed, but what she had heard had not been the beginning of either. (Susan was grim, perhaps even half-prepared.)

But the covering on the head bent at an impossible angle toward the shoulder was not a scarf; it was the drawn-tight hood of a man's parka. Willis! shrieked Celia soundlessly in the lightning-shot blackness of her brain, but a terrible telescoping process of knowledge had begun. She would not realize until later that she had guilt-created an avenger out of her past where none existed actively as such, that she had in effect fled where no one pursued, but she knew even before a shocking white light poured down on her there on the ice, with a haunted-looking woman in gray and a Priory employe behind it, that she had killed Jules Wain.

She did shriek aloud then, and they took her away and presently took Jules Wain away too, disclosing the tear-gas gun on which his body had fallen.

It was drawn from a tight-lipped Adelaide Wain that she had indeed let her late brother-in-law's discharged secretary, David Farrell, know the time and place of the wedding when he telephoned to ask, but that she had no idea that he would send this information, together with the newspaper clipping, to Jules's pathologically jealous ex-wife—hadn't even known, she insisted, that Farrell was still in touch with the woman ten years after the divorce. The former Teresa da Cunha was in and out of mental institutions during that period; ironically, the Wain level of society had chosen to interpret Jules's explanation of instability—the truth—as a cloak for alcoholism.

Early on that prewedding evening, in spite of the changes brought about by years and illness, Adelaide had recognized the woman in the lobby and, knowing her to be fully capable of violence, told Jules. He in turn tried to reach Celia at her hotel to warn her not to go out and to let no one in—and there Adelaide Wain's knowledge of events ended.

It was where the jury's troubles began. Celia said calmly that late that afternoon she had received an anonymous letter so disgusting that she had burned it at once but, upon reflection, decided to go to The Priory and consult Jules about it. Once there, she had begun to feel that it was foolish to cast this cloud over their wedding, and had taken a walk outside to think it over.

"In fourteen-degree weather?"

"I was warmly dressed, and I have always enjoyed walking."

"With a tear-gas gun."

"Certainly. My fiancé had bought it for me after an incident near my home and insisted upon my carrying it."

Then came the recital of the man looming up in the dark, indescribably menacing on the heels of the anonymous letter, and Celia's own instinct of self-defense. "I was terrified when he fell. I had no idea that there were steps there. I went down to see if he were badly injured, if there was something I could do before I went for help, and then, . . . and then —"

(*Then* she realized that Jules had occupied the wing chair, belated in his recognition of her scarfed, ski-suited back view because she was the last person he expected to see at The Priory that evening, and gone out after her and even called to her . . . He had ordered a taxi, it was revealed later—to go to Celia's hotel?—and was presumably waiting for it well out of sight of his unpredictable ex-wife.)

Was it conceivable, the jury had to ask themselves, that a woman would wilfully kill her wealthy fiancé for no discernible reason on the very eve of their wedding? There were countless recorded cases of tragic error: farmers waking up in the night to take rifles and shoot their own sons, wives surprised out of sleep dispatching their husbands.

Celia went free.

Having as it did the magic elements of money, social status, and fashionable setting, the trial was widely reported. It unearthed Mrs. Cannon, and then Mrs. Stryker, and a reluctant Mrs. Stevenson; there was even a newspaper photograph of the Bridgeport tenement, although all this was ruled out as having no bearing. On a sweltering New Jersey afternoon in late June, a thirsty man in a bar remarked, "Ask me, she got away with murder. Good thing it wasn't a poisoning case."

With this lure cast out, he waited until his drinking companion bought him another beer. "Remember that Lambert who was a character witness, said she'd never hurt a fly? William, Willis, something like that. Set up the Lambert Lounge over on Twelfth Street, kind of a tacky place, you know what I mean, a little rough sometimes, but the food isn't bad. I don't know if he married her or what, but she works there as a waitress . . ."

Ursula
ent